Class Acts
Short Stories for Teenagers

Linda Jones Simmons

Front Cover Photos at
Monrovia High School, Monrovia, CA

Left to right standing:
Aranza Osorio, Katelin Casner, Dherik Ahmad, Nicholas Miranda,
Tanya Galvan, Bradley Carels, Alicia Rangel

Left to right seated:
George Richardson, Gabriel Martinez

Façade with Bell Tower, Monrovia High School

Photos by Linda Jones Simmons

ISBN-13: 9781490446837
ISBN-10: 1490446834

To Robert Montes and his Monrovia High School Fifth Period English I Class, spring of 2012, with gratitude for the feedback and interest in this "Meet the Author" literary project

Contents

Preface

*C*lass Acts is written for teenagers. Not that others wouldn't enjoy the stories or learn something from them, but the content of this collection deals with issues pertaining specifically to adolescents. Though this is a work of fiction, the genesis for each story comes from encounters with students during my thirty-six-year teaching career. Any similarity in names among these characters to real-life subjects is purely coincidental.

I consider this work a companion piece for my nonfiction book, *This Was Meant to Be – How Loss and Vulnerability Generate Passion and Success*. Though a great deal of ground was covered in that work, there were still more stories to be told, additional lessons to be learned, and most importantly, numerous teenagers to serve who might have a preference for fiction rather than nonfiction.

There have been remarkable changes in adolescents over the decades, most of which are technology driven. Along these lines, there are many advantages available today that unfortunately, were unavailable when I was in school. How did Americans ever survive the use of typewriters instead of computers, carbon paper for copies because copy machines hadn't been invented yet, one telephone per home, and no television until the late forties? Somehow we did.

Despite the advances of technology, there has been a downside leading to the depersonalization of how we interact with one another. It is common to see two kids standing side-by-side texting one another on their cell phones. Will eye contact soon go the way of the typewriter, carbon paper, and the horse and buggy? Many times I've sat in restaurants observing one person staring blankly ahead while the companion is chattering away on a cell phone. Really? How did people *ever* get through a meal before the cell phone was invented? How many times have we called a business only to get caught in an endless maze of menu choices? There seems to be a love-hate relationship with the phone these days. We can't stop chatting with friends while shopping, eating, sitting in a movie, waiting for a doctor appointment, or sitting in class, yet we cannot connect with a human being when we wish to execute a business transaction or query.

In addition to technology's downside, there has also been the demise in critical thinking related, in part, to technology. However, that's not the only culprit that has rendered changes in adolescent behavior.

What are some of these contributing factors? There are many that would fill another book, but here are a few: 1) The Dumbing Down of America, begun shortly after 1959, that solicits movement in education away from deep critical thought and authentic assessment to more superficial curricula and measurements of student achievement in academia. 2) The No Child Left Behind Act of 2001, a skills-based curriculum centered on teaching to frequently-administered benchmark and standardized tests, instituted by President George W. Bush and passed by Congress in 2001. 3) Visual and radio media where content is compressed into four to eight-minute sound bytes. 4) The demise of a reading culture with a corresponding inability to activate one's imagination for visualization. 5) The inability to read silently and comprehend what has been read. 6) Media distractions that entertain but do not foster deep critical thought. 7) Revisionist history resulting in an embarrassing lack of knowledge of our own country's history.

These, then, are but a few of the contributing factors to a loss in our ability to think, problem solve, and create. If any reader doubts me on this, look deeply into our dysfunctional Congress. Their inability to get things done is not merely a matter of differences in ideology or party politics; it is due to their inability to *think* and to problem solve. We hear slogans, such as "Throw the Bums Out!" in frustration regarding failure to do their jobs. However, even if all the "bums" were thrown out, would we simply vote in more of the same?

Young people need to know that all of our problems are not to be blamed on the economy, the inability of our politicians to lead, and the greed of people in power. We've been through much tougher economic times in the past and unfortunately, greed within the powerful ruling class will always be our nemesis. The point is, those are not excuses for lack of achievement.

Many of our nation's monumental masterpieces were created during a period in which the world was struggling through the Great Depression of the 1930s. These engineering feats included Hoover Dam constructed between 1931 and 1936, Mount Rushmore Memorial created between 1934 and 1939, San Francisco's Golden Gate Bridge begun in 1933 and finished in 1937, one of the Seven Modern Wonders of the World, and the

Empire State Building, 1930-1931, also one of the Seven Modern Wonders of the World. These were monumental achievements of engineering and artistic brilliance created during a decade when technology was no match for the technological advancements of today. Despite political differences and financial hardships, Americans always got things done with their indomitable can-do spirit. To put it plainly, our forefathers were not dumbed down. They were readers, critical thinkers, creators, and problem solvers who would weep were they privy to the current Congressional paralysis that is ravaging our country today. For them, hard times and political differences were not excuses for lack of achievement.

For your sake, it is my hope there will be enough critical thinkers among you to address some of our contemporary issues, the most pressing among them being our economy and crumbling infrastructure such as roads, bridges, electrical grids, and levees.

Why the history lesson in this preface for short stories? I want you young readers to *think* about your place in American history, for you are all a part of the fabric of this country. Will you allow yourselves to become dumbed down, numbed to the problems that need solving, or will you rise to the spirit of our can-do predecessors and make something of your lives as contributing members of society?

The adolescents depicted in these short stories represent the triumphs and failures typical among the young people who populated my life as teacher and now as teacher trainer. If any of these stories remind you of your own situations or those of others you know, perhaps they will enable you to better understand the curve balls life throws at us from time to time and how to cope with them.

For those of you who enjoy writing, you might try your hand at creating your own epilogues to "A Boy Without a Father," "A Girl Without a Father," "Summer School," and "Who Among You Would Serve?" If you don't like my endings, feel free to write your own! Above all, may you find this collection a worthwhile read.

Linda Jones Simmons

Pasadena, California

June 2013

A Boy Without a Father

———

Antonio was a stocky kid who stood at about five feet eight inches tall. He kept his head – or dome, as the boys called it – nearly clean-shaven. Antonio understood power and how to use it among his peers. He was the textbook alpha male: dominant, heavily laden with testosterone, controlling, and able to get numerous followers to do his bidding. In fact, he was so confident that he often overstepped his bounds with his teachers, a breach of protocol that often landed him in suspension either on or off campus.

Yes, Antonio was arrogant, dangerous, and sometimes ruthless. However, despite his obvious misgivings, he could be a likeable fellow with a sharp whit and quick mind. No drugs were taken by the boy, for he needed a lucid mind to wield power over his minions and to plan upcoming adventures that included tagging, playing war games with paint guns, beating up and terrorizing unsuspecting graveside mourners (called *wildings*) at the local cemetery, and showing prospective gang members, waiting to be jumped in, how to steal cars and bring back proof of thefts to gang headquarters. Spoils consisted of car parts such as ignition cylinders, batteries, radios, or anything else that could be quickly lifted and stowed in a getaway car, probably stolen as well.

His eighth grade teachers, especially the one whose car he stole for *his* jumping-in rite of passage, took a great interest in the boy as a last-ditch effort to save him from himself before moving on to high school. Despite his bravado and tendency to bully others, Antonio could not entirely hide his vulnerability. You see, Antonio had no father, no positive, strong male role model to mentor him through his adolescence. Furthermore, there was an uncomfortable aloofness between him and his mother, who spoke no English.

Antonio was typical of many children brought to this country against their will and having their lives severely interrupted. Like many, he was resentful of having been thrust into a foreign culture at an early age and having been expected to thrive in classes conducted in a language he didn't understand. There were kids who openly admitted refusing to speak their native language at home if their parents didn't make the effort to learn English. Then there was the pecking order with which to contend regarding animosity between the newly-arrived and formerly-arrived immigrants. One had to work one's way up the ladder for acceptance.

"I'll talk to my mother whenever she learns English," Antonio blurted out to Mr. Watanabe one day just before lunch. Mr. Watanabe, or Mr. W., as he was more commonly known, had simply asked the boy as he was leaving if his mom had received his progress report that had been recently sent through the mail.

"Nah, she can't read it, so that's *her* problem. If she wants to know what's going on in my life, she'll have to learn the language."

"From what I've heard about your after-hours indulgences, chances are your mother wouldn't want to know what's going on in your life."

"Yeah, whatever," he shrugged while reaching into his backpack and whipping out a small album of photos documenting tagged sites and some of their war games in progress. "Wanna see my pictures of our tagging spree from last weekend?" he asked, handing them over to Mr. W. No doubt about it, Antonio was proud of being a gang-banger and he took his photos everywhere as proof of his organizational skills and ability to attract followers, not to mention the devastation left in his wake.

Mr. W. glanced through the album, unimpressed and disgusted by such a waste of a young life. Then he set it aside. "So where do you see yourself five years from now after you leave high school?" his teacher wanted to know.

"I'm gonna go into the military. I want to learn more about technology and play war games for real."

"So the possibility of being in real warfare sounds like a game to you?"

"Yeah, I guess so. You get to kill people legally." Referring to Antonio as a depressed boy with pent-up anger would be an understatement.

"Well, listen up; here is some eye-opening information: Your application to enlist in *any* branch of the military would end up in the circular file, unread, because your academic record is terrible. To use your vernacular, it sucks. Working with paintballs is a far cry from the highly technical skills required of service men and women in order to engage in combat or even to support those on the front lines. So far, you've proven yourself an academic flake, choosing to produce nothing of value. Furthermore, the photo album you so proudly display and your 1.20 GPA would serve as a pretty lame résumé for any employment opportunity outside the confines of your gang affiliations."

One could always count on Mr. W. for straight talk. That's why the kids respected him so much. Aside from being a fine science teacher, he was like a second father for those who came from stable homes and served as surrogate father for those who came from fatherless homes.

This was indeed news to Antonio. "You mean I have to become a nerd to get into the Marines? What if people see me carrying books around and stuff? I'll lose all credibility with my –"

"With your gang?" interrupted Mr. W. "You'll lose your street creds?"

"Yeah, that," mumbled a stunned Antonio who was trying to take in the horrible disclosure Mr. W. had just laid upon him.

"If you want to be in the military, I would advise raising your GPA, especially if you don't intend on going to college. These days, the all-voluntary military can afford to be highly selective. You'll be competing among college graduates as well as those who try to enter with only a high school diploma. At best, you might qualify for latrine duty. Right now, you are not even eligible for a middle school diploma. You have a 1.20 GPA. Would you be willing to put your life in the hands of a slacker such as yourself on the battlefield?" He didn't wait for an answer. "I don't think so."

Antonio sat mute, deep in thought, his dreams already shattered of entering the military without having to so much as lift a finger for acceptance into the branch of his choice. Yes, this was a bright, but ignorant homeboy who knew little of the world outside the confines of his small circle of gang-bangers.

"So how do I do that?"

"Do what?" asked Mr. W.

"Get my GPA up to a 3.00."

"Well, for starters, you come prepared to work each day. You study. You do your homework. In short, you focus on things other than wildings, tagging, war games, and whatever else you and your buddies do to waste your lives away."

"I gotta be seen carrying books?"

"Oh, gee. That would be a shame, wouldn't it? People are getting their heads chopped off throughout the Middle East and displayed on You Tube while Antonio is seen carrying a book or two to class. My, God, Antonio, pick up a newspaper once in a while or follow some news on TV and learn what's going on in the world. If you want to be a warrior – most likely in the Middle East – you need to learn how you, too, might get your head chopped off and your torso dragged through the streets."

Antonio looked startled. "Things are that bad over there?"

"Only for hundreds of years," he retorted sarcastically. "Wake up and get your head out of the sand. Then you'll learn how ridiculous your fear of being seen carrying books is. People in some parts of the world would – and have – literally died for an education, yet you choose to blow off your opportunities."

Still determined not to be seen carrying books, but willing to make a few concessions, Antonio was ready to cut a deal with Mr. W. "What if I hide my books somewhere in here and come in after school to do my homework?"

Mr. W. could barely keep from laughing at the lad's determination to hide any evidence of achievement. "All right. We can do that. However, you do remember that my grades are posted; there are no secrets in this class. Just be prepared for what others may say when they see your rise on the grade scale."

"I'll deal with people who make fun of me."

"By beating them up? Did it ever occur that you could use your gift for leadership in a positive way? If you told many of your buddies to jump off a balcony, they'd probably do it. By the same token, if you encouraged them to wise up and start studying so they could graduate with a decent GPA, they'd do that, too. No one in the past has ever enjoyed repeating the eighth grade. The slackers would listen to you."

"You think so?"

"I know so. You already wield considerable influence over your peers, so why not lead them down a different path? Right now, you're behaving like a loser, despite your intelligence and leadership abilities. I guarantee they will follow you wherever you choose to lead them."

"Hmmmmm. Okay, I'll give it a try. We'll see how it goes this semester. I'm not making any promises beyond that."

"If you maintain the desire to serve in the U.S. Military, you won't have to promise beyond that. Your passion will overtake you and you will no longer be satisfied with your current academic status. You now have a positive goal. What could be more honorable than wanting to serve your country? Get a hold of some books and magazines dealing with the military to keep that interest alive. Stoke the fires, so to speak."

"All right, Mr. W. I'll give it a try. Just make sure you keep my books hidden away."

"Is that an order, or do you want to think of another way to phrase that last sentence? I'm not one of your underlings. News flash: I'm the adult authority figure in charge here, so don't you ever forget that. Let's try again."

Antonio rolled his eyes, "Will you please keep my books hidden away so nobody can find them?"

"Once more without the eye roll. Just look in my eyes and make the request."

Antonio did as instructed.

"*Much better!* See? You're already on the right track. One of the many things you'll learn in the military is to respect authority. You may as well start here and now. Just think of us teachers as your commanding officers."

"Thanks, Mr. W. I'll try to remember that." He gathered his things and looked around the room for an appropriate area to hide his books. Satisfied that the right place had been selected, he put the one book that was hidden under his jacket in its special place. "See you after school."

"I'll be here. Have a good afternoon." Mr. W. began preparing his room for the next period.

As the weeks passed, the layers of hardness began to erode and peel away. Antonio became Mr. W.'s class clown, letting his gift for comedic timing and harmless pranks lighten the spirit not only in Mr. W.'s class, but also in his other periods. There were instances of backsliding, resulting in a quick removal from the room so that Mr. W. could immediately "dress him down." True to character, Mr. W. did not mince words during his renewed efforts to leave no doubt that he was the "commanding officer" in charge.

During the last week of school, Antonio dropped by Mr. W.'s room to turn in some work. Mr. W. had just finished calculating the GPAs for his students and couldn't wait to share the glad tidings with his star pupil. "You're going to love this news, Antonio. I've just finished calculating everyone's GPAs and yours is a 3.50. Congratulations! I'm very proud of you, for you had to overcome a lot to get this far."

Antonio's face brightened a bit, but it wasn't the look of elation Mr. W. had hoped to see.

"What's wrong? I thought you'd be leaping for joy. You're on the right track now and have established good habits for your high school years."

"Nobody's coming to my graduation," he mumbled seemingly unaware of Mr. W.'s commendations. His voice was hollow and emotionless. "I brought the tickets home, but nobody wanted to use them." He tossed them on a nearby desk. "You can give 'em away. Maybe someone else's family can use 'em." Shades of his old hardness emerged as a familiar measure of self-defense to keep signs of vulnerability at bay. It had been some time since Mr. W. had seen The Look of Hardness and he was both stunned and saddened. "Screw them. I hate them," Antonio blurted.

"Oh, God, Antonio, don't go there . . . not after all you've accomplished. Please don't go there. It is a tragedy that things have not gone well in your family life, but only you can rise above those circumstances and save yourself. What you decide now will most likely determine your life's course."

"Why should I care if they don't?"

"Because unlike them, you have a goal, an honorable mission to accomplish. You have proven your ability to become one of the best Marines our country has to offer. Don't give up that dream. It's what has given you direction and motivation to succeed this year. Don't throw that away. You'll graduate with your head held high – a student on the honor roll no less – knowing that we here are all very proud of what you've accomplished. Please don't let your dysfunctional family take that away from you."

Antonio left the room, head down and shoulders slumped, without uttering a response. During the final two days of class, he appeared sullen, moody, though not disruptive. While his classmates busied themselves signing yearbooks and sharing memories of their middle school days and their hopes for the years to come, Antonio sat mute. Finally, on the last day, the tears began to flow. Mr. Watanabe approached him and whispered, "Would you like to leave the room for a bit?" Antonio shook his head. Instead, he sat very still and cried, head unbowed, heedless of the students' chatter surrounding him.

The fact that Antonio no longer tried to hide his vulnerability signaled a great leap forward in maturation as far as Mr. Watanabe was concerned. Antonio was beyond caring what others thought of him. *How fragile our lives are,* thought Mr. W., looking out over his soon-to-be ninth graders. *Anything could happen to these kids over the summer and during the next four years. It's anybody's guess as to whether or not Antonio will keep his dream alive and make something of himself.*

At the graduation dance, Antonio was evasive, making a pointed effort to avoid his teachers who had grown so fond of him. Leaving the cocoon of middle school where people had taken such an intense interest in him was just too painful. For the first time in his life, he had felt genuine attachments to something positive. He even allowed himself the luxury of being nurtured by his teachers and football coaches. However, the bonds would soon be forever broken. With the ties severed, he would be out on his own, starting up the ladder again as a ninth grader, an underling without a voice in the normal pecking order among adolescents. Only he could control his destiny by keeping the dream alive of joining the Marines.

Mr. Watanabe wanted to approach him, to wish him well, but he sensed that would be the wrong thing to do. Antonio was clearly having separation anxieties, for his body language revealed a very fragile state. To approach him would have run the risk of causing another emotional breakdown and he wanted to spare Antonio such a show of vulnerability on grad night.

Instead, Mr. W. stood his distance from the graduates, some dancing, some hugging their teachers or crying in their arms, others tearing up in the arms of their friends, while the remainder continued eating and chatting in animated tones. That was the bitter sweetness of helping kids move on to the next milestone in their lives. You grow to love them. Then they fly away. Though painful to experience, this is as it should be. As they get on with their lives, another group will emerge in September waiting to be taught and yes, wanting to be respected, nurtured and loved.

Epilogue

Over the next several years, Mr. Watanabe made occasional inquiries at the high school about Antonio. Indeed, he did graduate with honors and yes, he served two years in the military. During the beginning of his third year in Afghanistan, he stepped on a landmine, having rushed out to retrieve an injured victim before the enemy could get to him. He died of his injuries three days later.

Antonio had come a long way from days of aimless pursuits with his small-town homeboys so many years ago. He died fulfilling his dream of serving his country as a United States Marine. No one, not even his dysfunctional family, could deny him that distinction. He was laid to rest at Arlington National Cemetery while the colleague whose life he saved played *Taps* on a bugle from his wheelchair.

A Girl Without a Father

Allyson was as blonde and fair as a girl could be without having Albinism. Her curly shoulder-length hair was thick, nearly white; her eyes a pale Mediterranean blue. She was slight of build, shy and completely lacking in self-confidence. Allyson had been moved from foster care to foster care home, never residing in any one place for more than a couple of years at a time. At least one lucky break was in store for her in that she would remain with her current foster parents for all four years of high school.

To save face among her peers, Allyson created a fictitious history for herself and none was the wiser as far as she knew. The girl had told the story so many times, even she began to believe it: Her parents were killed in an automobile accident when she was very young. They were traveling from Southern California headed north up Highway 99 toward the San Joaquin Valley in Central California. The dense fog, known as "Tule fog" (pronounced **too**-lee) among the natives, was responsible for a freak accident causing a twelve-car pile up. This story was entirely believable among Californians familiar with the terrible weather conditions in the San Joaquin Valley during winter months. It was not uncommon to see these dreadful accidents played out on television during the evening news.

In truth, Allyson convinced herself this is what happened to her parents because the actual set of circumstances were just too painful to bear. In reality, her father was serving a life-without-parole sentence for having killed a fellow drunk in a barroom brawl. Shortly after his incarceration, her mother took off for parts unknown, leaving her with an aunt until she could be placed in foster care. Due to these unconscionable behaviors on the part of her wayward parents, Allyson was transformed into a deeply scarred throwaway child. What effect would all of this have during her most impressionable years of adolescence?

Despite the ups and downs of her hapless home life, Allyson was a model student and gifted pianist who accompanied the high school concert choir and chamber ensemble. Miss Ramirez, the vocal music director, allowed the budding musician to practice before and after school. Frequently, she would even practice during lunch. The choir room piano became *her* instrument, her lifeline to hours of escape from reality. Because she was so gifted in music, Miss Ramirez sought out a local piano teacher who agreed to give her *pro bono* lessons.

Her closest friend was Natalie Jones, a tall, slender African American member of the chamber ensemble. She, too, was a talented musician who studied privately with a professor from a nearby college. Natalie came from a well-to-do family of highly educated parents. Her father was an ophthalmologist and her mother was a physics professor. They placed a great deal of pressure upon their daughter to succeed academically, accepting nothing less than a 3.6 or higher GPA each semester. Though she loved her parents who worked hard to give her every advantage possible, she sometimes felt beaten down by academic pressures. Music, then, was her escape as it had been for Allyson, though for different reasons. Despite their contrary backgrounds and striking physical differences, they had much in common through their love of music and academic achievements.

Throughout their years of high school, Natalie looked after Allyson knowing that her friend had none of the advantages her parents had provided for her. Allyson felt a greater sense of belonging to Natalie's family because she was never with her series of foster parents long enough to bond with them. Though she was not mistreated by them, Allyson was convinced they remained indifferent toward her, accepting parentless teenagers such as herself into their homes, to get the monthly child support payments from Sacramento.

This, however, was not the case with the Grovers. Allyson was their fourth foster child and admittedly their favorite. They were getting along in years, however, so Allyson would probably be their last child. This made the enjoyment of having the gifted youth in their home even more bittersweet.

By the time both girls entered their senior year, Miss Ramirez encouraged them to apply for music scholarships to colleges of their choice. After four years of performances and recitals, their talents were legion in the community and among their adolescent peers. Miss Ramirez frequently programed them for piano-voice duets on her choir concerts whereby such pairings became a student body favorite for concerts and assemblies.

Despite their varied backgrounds, these two friends seemed to have the world by the tail with bright futures looming ahead. They set about filling out applications and creating those dreaded essays required by each college and university.

"Wouldn't it be great," mused Allyson, "if we could use one essay for all our applications?"

"Sure would," Natalie agreed. "I'm getting sick of writing these! I wonder if anybody actually reads them."

"Hopefully, they'll be more interested in our audition tapes than our essays. We want to be musicians, not writers."

Life proceeded as usual and by late February, the girls had received their notices. Though they were not accepted to the university of their first choosing, the news was still good: Natalie would be going to Columbia University in New York City, but her parents' combined income exceeded qualification for a scholarship. Allyson would attend Oberlin Conservatory of Music in Oberlin, Ohio with full scholarship and a part-time job awaiting her. The girls joyfully celebrated their prospects for a bright future with a small dinner party hosted by Natalie's parents.

Unfortunately, there was a darker secret life unfolding for Allyson that would eventually shock the living daylights out of everyone who knew her. You see, despite all her success, there was still one thing missing from her life: a father. This she wanted above all else and if she couldn't have one in a family setting, she'd find another way.

The one unfortunate act of kindness executed in all innocence by the Grovers was the purchase of a computer for their foster child. They thought it would be a useful tool for completing on-line research for school projects and she could take it to college with her, one less expense to worry about for this prospective college freshman.

While looking for love on the internet, Allyson hooked up with a forty-eight-year-old predator. He told her all the things she longed to hear: she was special; she could be "daddy's little girl" if only she would come to him; she was just about the cutest little thing walking the earth; he would be the perfect catalyst for her music career, no need for that college stuff; "I love you like I've never loved anyone before." The predatory drivel was sickening and endless; the man, Jack Wattleman, knew exactly what to say to stroke her ego and melt her heart. The vulnerable teenager was impervious to the thirty-year age difference between them; what mattered was the way he made her feel.

Had Allyson shared the dark parallel history with anyone before it got out of hand, she may have had a chance to withdraw from the web he wove for her. However, this cyber affair had been going on *sub rosa* for several months and by May, Allyson had become inextricably locked in the vise-like grasp of this pariah. She was committed to Jack, declaring her love for him in an endless stream of e-mails and phone calls. He was her Svengali who took over her life and nearly swallowed her whole as a wild animal eats its prey. The next step of course, would be their in-person encounter.

Allyson's secret life became exposed when her foster mom was cleaning her room. Allyson had accidentally left her cell phone on the desk and when it rang, Mrs. Grover answered the call, a purely reflexive reaction on her part. Besides, Allyson had given her no reason to suspect that anything of a sordid nature was going on in her life.

"Hello, Allyson?" came the mature, deep male voice at the end of the line.

"No, Allyson's at school. May I take a message?"

"No, I'll call later." A chill ran through Mrs. Grover for the voice sounded too mature for that of a teenage boy.

"Is this one of Allyson's friends from school?" She knew it wasn't but wanted to hear his adult voice again to confirm her suspicions.

"No, I'm not. I'll call later." Click.

Mrs. Grover's hands began to tremble. She was torn between invading Allyson's privacy by opening up her e-mails or simply questioning her when she got home from school. She decided to take the latter course of action.

When Allyson entered the house later that afternoon, Mrs. Grover called her into the living room, asking her to sit down.

"Allyson, I'm going to ask you a very serious question and I want an honest answer," Mrs. Grover began. Allyson hadn't been to her room yet, so she may not have remembered leaving her phone on the desk.

"Sure. What is it?"

"Today, when I was cleaning the room, your phone rang. You forgot to take it with you today and without thinking, I answered it. The call was from an older man, obviously not a boy your age. I figured if it were a harmless call from the school office or from your uncle, he would have identified himself. I asked him if he'd like to leave a message but he said he'd call later. What's going on and who is this man?"

Allyson's cheeks and neck flushed a deep pink. She sat motionless, not knowing how to begin.

"I'm waiting for an explanation," Mrs. Grover prompted.

"Well, that's my private business. Why do I have to tell you who he is?"

"Because you live here, that's why, and we're responsible for you so long as you're with us. You're a dependent, so it *is* our business who you associate with."

"If I tell you, you'll get mad and send me away."

"Of course we would never do that. Whatever the problem is, we can work it out. Besides, you're about to leave for college, so you'll be turning yourself out. You'll be starting a whole new life in Oberlin with an incredible future in store for you."

"Sorry, I'm not going . . . to Oberlin. I'm –"

"You're *not* going to Oberlin?" Mrs. Grover interrupted. "You're *not* going to the conservatory? Please tell me you're joking!"

"I'm not. Jack says he loves me and I love him. We've been writing and phoning back and forth for about six months. He sent me an airline ticket to meet him in Chicago. Then we'll fly to Bangkok together and tour the Orient."

Mrs. Grover wanted to scream, to shake the girl to her senses, but she forced herself to remain calm. She needed to get as much information as possible out of her in case legal action needed to be taken. "How old is this Jack person and what's his last name?" was all she could manage.

"Jack Wattleman . . . forty-eight."

"Oh, honey, you're looking for a father, not a boyfriend. He's practically old enough to be your grandfather for heaven's sake! This man's a predator, a loser, who couldn't make it with women closer to his own age, so he stalks much younger, vulnerable girls like you who'll believe anything he tells them."

Allyson was adamant in her belief that she had found true love, never mind that she didn't know what he did for a living, or why he wanted to take her to Bangkok.

"Do you know what this man, Jack, does for a living?" The words *Slave Trade* came immediately to mind. *He sells young girls into bondage. That's what I'll bet he does for a living,* she thought.

"No. I never asked. If he could afford to send me a ticket to Chicago and take us overseas, I assume he's doing all right financially."

"And do you know where you'll be staying in Chicago? In Bangkok? Anywhere?"

"No. I figure he'll tell me when he makes all the arrangements."

"Allyson, do you know *anything* about Bangkok?"

"Not really."

"It's the capital of Thailand, a densely-populated urban city in Southeast Asia, well known for sex trafficking and prostitution. Because the city is so crowded, it's easy for people to engage in sex crimes and human slave trade because they're not likely to be tracked down."

"Well, I'm not worried. I'm sure Jack will protect me from all of that."

"Nevertheless, you mustn't make a move with this man until you've gathered as much information as you can about him and where he's taking you. Have you told Natalie yet or anyone else at school?"

"No, not yet. I was waiting until after graduation to tell her along with some other friends."

"And your generous piano teacher who has invested so much time on your behalf without charging us a dime for his services because he believed in you and your talent? Your choir director, who made piano practicing time available for you and showcased your talent for four years? And Oberlin Conservatory? Just when were you planning on telling them?"

"Probably the same time . . . after graduation. I'll write Oberlin next week so they can give the scholarship to somebody else."

"So to run off with this pariah, you're willing to break the hearts of all the people who took you under their wings, trying to help you create a better future for yourself? You're willing to throw all that away and ruin your life for a predator?"

"That's not true! He's *not* a predator! We love each other and . . . and . . .who said he'd ruin my life anyway?"

"*I'm* telling you, he'll ruin your life," Mrs. Grover nearly screamed while pointing an accusatory finger at Allyson.

"Jack promised to help me with my career in music," Allyson responded with a bit less resolve.

"From Bangkok? Apparently, you're missing a very important piece of history here: People come from Asia to make their mark *here* in the United States. *This* is where performers want to come to build their careers. I doubt you'll find a single American who has flown to Bangkok to launch a career as a concert pianist . . . just a guess on my part."

Allyson shrugged her shoulders. "Well, we won't stay in Bangkok. We'll move around."

She clearly had lost her senses . . . hadn't thought anything through. In her desperation to run into the arms of a father figure, she abandoned all thoughts of practicality, of reason.

"And the piano? Will you be moving around Asia with your own piano?"

"I don't know," she sighed, running her hand through her curly hair. "He promised me he'd take care of all that stuff," she answered with a little less resolve in her voice.

"You know, there are kids who would kill for your talent, your smarts, and the opportunities you are about to throw away. I'm begging you to give this some serious consideration before you go running off to Chicago, Bangkok, Mars or wherever you're headed with this man."

"My mind's made up. We really love each other a lot and I'm ready for some adventure."

"Adventure? Oh, you'll find adventure all right. Before you contact Jack again, you might want to Google "slave trade" in Bangkok, other parts of Thailand, or the Philippines so you'll get a peek at what's probably in store for you. You're eighteen so unfortunately, we have no legal right to stop you from running away. However, we had hoped that by giving you a stable home life, you would make better choices with your opportunities."

Allyson slowly stood up asking, "Are we done here?"

"Oh, yes. We are *so* done here," was all the response Mrs. Grover could muster. When her husband returned home from work, she recounted the grim news.

"You know, I'm deeply saddened, but not surprised," he responded. "Girls without fathers often have a very poor track record because they spend their lives deep into adulthood looking for an elusive father figure. Predators are on to young vulnerable girls and boys suffering from low self-esteem. Men like Jack know exactly what makes these kids tick and how to manipulate them to become a part of their lives."

"They ought to require high school kids to take a course on stuff like this. It's a damn shame they don't," complained Mrs. Grover.

Allyson was typical of over-adaptive adopted children imbued with the "perfect child complex" by being good to a fault in hopes of pleasing everyone, especially their adoptive parents. She had been the perfect student, friend, foster child, and now the perfect victim of a pathological predator who made her offers she just couldn't refuse for fear of hurting his feelings.

"I feel so stupid for not seeing this coming," cried the teary-eyed wife. "Allyson gave us no reason, left no signs she had been leading a double life. Aside from her musical talent, she has proven herself to be a gifted actress, for she has certainly succeeded in pulling the wool over *my* eyes. Had I not answered her phone, I wonder when she would have told us? It breaks my heart that she's giving up her scholarship. What a waste of a life to run off with that monster!"

"Well, maybe this should be our last foster child. We've taken in four so far and all but Allyson have made positive choices with their lives after high school. I guess three out of four isn't bad, but this one . . . this Allyson had such extraordinary talent . . . so much going for her."

The Grovers were devastated for the road their fourth foster child had chosen. In retrospect, they wished they could have benefitted from training on picking up cues when secret lives of kids are in progress. They discussed how foster parents ought to be required to "take a course on stuff like this." One thing they did learn from this experience: Children are masters at masking their feelings. Because open communication was not maintained between them and Allyson, it was easy for her to live her secret life.

One by one, Allyson severed ties after graduation with the people who had done so much for her and who, at one time, had meant a great deal to her. However, it was easier for her to let go of them than it was for them to realize she would be out of their lives forever. Because she never benefitted from any deep love and affection from what should have been her first and most important mentors, her parents, she never learned to bond with people the way others did who had come from a stable, healthy family environment. The Grovers tried to provide that stability for her, but their efforts were in vain.

The seeds for the capacity to trust and to show and receive genuine affection had never been sewn into the fabric of Allyson's childhood foundation. Running away with Jack would not change any of that, for the beleaguered pianist could not possibly know how to bond with a man thirty years her senior, even if he swore to love and protect her for the rest of her life. She simply lacked the life skills necessary to survive on her own in a normal relationship let alone one with a predator.

Allyson's lifelong passion had been music, the only element she could trust, the one area that made her feel like she was not worthless. But how did she feel away from the piano? Not even her musical and academic accomplishments could ease the pain fraught with self-loathing caused by the abandonment of her biological parents. She looked to Jack Wattleman who would surely exorcise her inner demons.

On the morning of her departure, the Grovers bade her a tearful farewell from their home. They did not drive her to the airport; they wanted no part of what they deemed to be a dangerous and uncertain future. Instead, Allyson used some of her graduation money for a Prime Time Shuttle ride to LAX where she would catch her flight bound for Chicago's O'Hare International Airport. Had she been bound for Oberlin, Ohio, the departure scenario would have been an entirely different affair. The Grovers would have gladly planned a road trip to Oberlin with their foster child, proudly helping her settle into college life. These good people genuinely cared for the girl and always had her best interests at heart. However, a joyful start for a bright future was not meant to be.

"Will you at least promise to write and let us know how you're doing?" asked Mr. Grover while the driver loaded her luggage into the back of the van.

"I promise. Don't worry about me. I'll be fine."

"Take care. We love you," was all they could manage.

They wanted to hug her, but Allyson moved away and stepped into the blue and yellow van without looking back. As the Super Shuttle sped off, Mr. Grover looked woefully at his wife, saying, "This move almost feels to me like a death wish. I have a horrible feeling we'll never see or hear from her again."

Indeed, they never did.

Friends with Benefits

Who was Angela kidding? Didn't her family, high school counselor, and friends warn her that she was on a self-destructive path? Her parents divorced at a crucial time in her life. She was about to enter tenth grade, a time when girls need a stable, fatherly influence in their lives to countermand those raging hormones so prevalent among adolescents, male and female.

She had always been close to her dad, a burly, jovial man who found humor and joy in every seemingly insignificant act she and her brother performed. During her freshman year, however, a malaise fell over the family when her parents began drifting apart. At first, there was just sporadic bickering between them, but as time progressed, their periods of alienation grew more frequent and lasted for longer periods of time.

Angela and her older brother, Kevin, who was in the eleventh grade, were very close and they talked frequently about the impending doom their family was facing.

"Kevin, what will become of us if Mom and Dad get a divorce? If Dad remarries and starts another family, how will Mom support us? I'm really scared."

"I don't think Dad would ever abandon us financially. He earns a good living with his construction company so I can't imagine that he'd skip out on child support," Kevin tried to reassure her.

"Yeah, but what if he does? Then what'll we do?"

"We'll get jobs and help Mom out. Let's just see what's going to happen before we worry about all the 'what-ifs.' We'll work things out."

"I wish I had your confidence," she sighed. "You always were so optimistic, just like Dad."

He put his arm around her shoulder and coaxed, "C'mon. Let's go downstairs to the driveway and shoot some hoops. We'll get those endorphins – my new science word of the day – circulating and we'll feel better in no time."

But Angela didn't feel better. As she had feared, her parents divorced, though her father never missed child support payments. For that, at least, she could be grateful. Her mom was working two jobs to make ends meet and Kevin was caught up with school, a part-time job, his own friends, and athletic activities.

In short, nobody at home noticed what was happening to Angela. Visits with her father occurred more infrequently, for he became increasingly involved with his new family life. Angela was not much different from many of her fatherless peers suffering from the abandonment of a parent. Like them, she was riddled with guilt and longing for her family as it once was. She was ravaged by such thoughts as, *Was it something Kevin and I did that drove him away? Are we not as good as his new family? What could we have done differently to keep him here?* Of course, there was nothing she and her brother could have done to keep their family intact, for the problems were between two parents, not two children. However, at this stage in her life, she was incapable of proper reasoning, so she placed much of the blame upon herself for her broken family that had become fractured, atomized.

As a result, she was bound for trouble. When girls can no longer find approval and guidance from a strong male presence in the family, they will seek it elsewhere, and this is what Angela did as a means of self-preservation.

The weeks slipped by, moving her into a mild depression. She began drifting away from her childhood friends and becoming increasingly involved with Jason, a junior in her Spanish class. Jason was her answer, so she thought. He was attentive, attractive, caring, and one more thing: He was a friend with benefits, her first such friend. He was her rock, her go-to soft place when she needed a welcome source of intimacy.

One afternoon, they plopped down on a couch at his parents' house and began watching television. They were about to switch from the Dr. Phil Show to the E! Channel so they could catch up on the latest Hollywood gossip. However, when they heard the show was featuring a sexually active teenage couple appearing on stage with both sets of parents, they stopped mid-click and settled back to watch the drama unfold.

Predictably, both sets of parents were concerned for their fifteen-year-old children's promiscuity. After Dr. Phil heard everybody's side of the issue, he asked a question that must have shaken the teens to their core. It proved to be a turning point for the girl. The question was posed first to the boy: "How long do you want this relationship to last?"

The boy innocently answered, "Oh, about another six months I guess." The girl was visibly shaken, devastated. When Dr. Phil turned the same question to her, she assumed their relationship would perhaps lead to marriage. How could she have been so naïve? The audience gasped; the parents gasped, but Dr. Phil was not surprised. He knew exactly what their responses would be, having worked with similar cases and knowing that females are typically more emotionally invested in their casual sex partners than males are. The tearful teen on the stage was proof of this. She had entirely misread the boy's intentions, thinking he would care about her if she gave herself over to him. How wrong she was! In the boy's eyes, she was nothing more than one who turns tricks with no strings attached. On the other hand, she declared that she had learned her lesson and would not make the same mistakes again.

Jason was not bothered by what they had just witnessed. In fact, he was prepared not to give it a second thought. He reached for the remote but she placed her hand firmly over his to prevent a channel change. After wresting the remote from him, Angela turned off the television. Then she took a long look at him.

"What?" he asked innocently. "Why did you turn off the TV and why are you staring at me?"

"That couple isn't us, is it? I mean, our relationship will last longer than six months, right?" she asked with uncertainty.

He blinked, startled by her question, genuinely surprised by her assumption that they were in a secure long-term relationship. "It all sounds pretty standard to me. I mean, that's what FWB is . . . just hooking up for a good time and a little action. I thought you understood that."

"No, no I didn't . . . have any idea. You were my first . . . um . . . You must think I'm an idiot and I sure am. How could I have been so stupid?"

"Well, then, you ought to talk to your girlfriends about FWB. You'd be surprised how many girls and guys are into it. There's no commitment or strings attached . . . just fun hooking up. What's not to like about that?"

"What's not to like about that? Are you *kidding me?* Next time you hook up with someone, try being honest about what you want from a girl. Your reaction to the show took me by surprise and left me feeling used, that's all. I completely misunderstood our relationship."

In Angela's frustration, she was not making clear connections between her own situation with Jason and their differing expectations. Adding to her confusion and annoyance with him was his blank stare. He had no clue regarding the point she was trying to make about her feelings and why she felt duped.

Angela stood up and backed away from him, reaching for her purse. "I think I've had enough of friends with benefits for now. Maybe we'd better stop seeing each other until we're clear about what we expect of one another." She paused to take one last look at Jason whereupon she vanished out the door.

"Suit yourself," the still-puzzled boy responded blandly flipping through channels, not even bothering to look up when she left. He went to the kitchen and got himself a snack. Then he settled into a rerun of his favorite television show, *CSI.*

As for Angela, she finally got it after gaining clarity from the Dr. Phil Show. She also grew to understand there were more positive ways of filling the void left by an absent father.

Though this knowledge didn't make it easier accepting the loss of someone considered to be a close friend, she would survive. After all, hadn't she lived through her parents' divorce? The loss of innocence deeply saddened her, but Jason was not entirely to blame. She had enjoyed his company and their intimacy as much as he had. Her walk home was filled with the bittersweet memories of a friendship that was not meant to last.

A Father's Disappointment

Emily McPherson and Lakisha Washington had been best friends since kindergarten. There is nothing they hadn't experienced as BFFs (Best Friends Forever), including sharing dreams, occasional quarreling, and telling each other their most private secrets and fantasies. Both came from fine two-parent homes, but even kids from the best of families can sometimes run amok. The girls were seniors heading toward their last semester of high school and "senioritis" had settled in with a vengeance.

Because all college applications had been submitted along with transcripts and SAT results from their junior year, they planned on simply coasting from December through the end of their last semester. Their classes weren't particularly challenging, so with minimal effort, they could slide through with Bs and Cs. "No problem," they agreed.

One morning during art class, Emily slipped a note to Lakisha that read: "How 'bout we cut out of here during lunch and spend the afternoon at the Arcadia Mall? I'm sooooooo bored!"

Lakisha wrote back: "Awesome. Let's do it!"

As soon as the lunch bell rang, they fled to the student parking lot, got into Emily's car, and headed for Arcadia. When they entered Macy's, they made their way to the teen clothing department and began sorting through skirts and blouses, heedless of the security guard standing nearby. Emily plucked a pricey ensemble off the rack and wondered out loud – though not too loud – "Do you suppose we could take this blouse and skirt without anyone seeing us?"

Lakisha was shocked. They had gotten into minor mischief through the years, but had never entertained thoughts of stealing. Her brown eyes clouded with anger as she sputtered, "Y-y-you can't be serious! Are you *crazy*, Girl? I'll tell a saleslady if you take anything from here," she threatened while looking nervously about. She was furious with her friend. What had come over her?

"If you do, Lakisha, you're walking home," Emily hissed. "Remember, we came in *my* car." Lakisha glared at her but said nothing as she turned on her heel and strutted away. Finding herself alone, Emily hastily stuffed the red plaid skirt and white blouse into the large purse she was carrying. She headed casually toward the escalator, sneaking furtive glances, checking for any suspicious bystanders as she continued on her way. It didn't occur to her to look for Lakisha, left on her own for a ride home.

The security guard, who had been watching the girls, tapped Emily on the shoulder and demanded that she remove the garments from her purse. "Young lady, just where do you think you're going with those clothes?" A tiny vein was pulsating on the right side of his neck as he continued to stare down at her from his six-foot frame.

"I-I was going to pay for them," she stammered lamely, looking fearfully up at him. By now her pulse was racing and the palms of her hands were sweating profusely.

"Then why did you have the clothes in your hand bag?" he snapped. "If you are intending to pay for them, I'll walk you to a register where the clerk can ring up the sale while I wait."

She peered inside her wallet. A five-dollar bill peered back at her. "Um, I-I d-don't h-have enough money to pay for these. Sorry. I'll never try this again. Please let me go," she begged.

"Not so fast. You're coming up to the security office with me and we're going to call one of your parents. Is your father at work?"

"Um . . . y-yes."

"Give me his number and I'll call him. Always works best when a parent has to leave work to pick up a troublesome kid."

With one hairy hand, he guided her toward the elevator, on their way upstairs to the security office. Emily had never stolen anything before and although frightened, she was also angry for having gotten caught her first time shoplifting.

My parents are going to kill me, the bored teen-turned-shoplifter thought. *They'll never trust me again with the car.*

When the officer got a hold of Emily's father, he reported that his daughter had been apprehended for shoplifting and that she would be prosecuted for petty theft. Mr. McPherson came right over to the security office. After all the appropriate paperwork had been filed, Emily was released to the custody of her father. The walk from the office to the car seemed like an eternity. The worst part of the walk was the eerie silence between them, for once outside, her heart-broken father uttered not a word.

Ever the gentleman, he walked her to the passenger side of his beige Chrysler van, opened the door, and motioned for her to enter. Emily saw the tears of disappointment streaming down his cheeks. That was the first time she had ever seen her father cry and it broke her heart to have made him so miserable. *He must be so ashamed of me and embarrassed. I don't know what got into me. No matter how bored I get, I'll never cut class again,* she vowed.

The December chill in the air made her shiver not only from the cold, but also with regret and anguish over what she had done. *God, how I have broken his heart!* She wanted to die right then and there.

At this point, it was five in the evening. They drove in silence for a long while, heading west toward the Pasadena Freeway. The disconsolate daughter was dying to know where her father was taking her, but she didn't dare ask. They drove toward Los Angeles, passing the familiar off-ramps that seemed to fly past in familiar order: Fair Oaks, Orange Grove Boulevard, Via Mariposa . . . a seemingly endless stream of exits. By the time they arrived in Los Angeles, she was getting a sense of what her father had in mind. They headed to where long lines of vagrants and homeless people were filing out of one of the soup kitchens. Others were setting out their frayed blankets and assorted dirty, pitiful possessions for the evening. Nightfall was upon them and the air grew increasingly damp and chilly.

Nothing could have prepared Emily for what her father did next: He pulled over to the curb and handed his daughter his watch. He then said, "This will hurt me more than it will hurt you. I want you to get out of the van and walk east for ten minutes. I will meet you at the corner of 6th and Gladys by the Hospitality Kitchen."

In disbelief, his daughter stared at him. Blinking back the tears she whimpered, "Y-you must be kidding! I don't even know where 6th and Gladys is."

"Ask someone; you'll find it. We're not far from there. Now get going."

His beleaguered daughter opened the door, terrified of mingling with the sordid clusters of humanity clutching their tattered clothing about them. Her father was serious about showing her what happens to some people who throw away opportunities for a good education and the advantages of fine upbringing. There was no choice but for Emily to leave the van and take her chances with a walk through the central city ghetto of L.A.'s Skid Row. After seeing her father's hurt, tear-stained face, she figured a walk through this part of town would be more bearable than witnessing the misery she had caused him. Upon leaving the van, he simply stated, "Today, you are no better than some of these people and for what you did, this is where you belong. This is where you'll end up if you continue to steal and get in trouble with the law."

Then he disappeared through the inky darkness, leaving her alone, filled with dread and shame and eventually, sorrow for the lost souls who populated the streets where she walked. Her focus shifted away from her own misery to that of the homeless. By the time Emily approached 6th and Gladys, she had spotted the vehicle with her father awaiting her arrival. She paused long enough to give a homeless passerby the five-dollar bill in her wallet. It seemed like decades ago since she had last seen it peering back at her while the security guard who called her bluff stood nearby.

When father and daughter reconnected, the ride home was as hushed as the trip into Los Angeles, but somehow, the silence was different. Emily sat beside her father shivering from the cold and crying inconsolably. He let her stew in her despair while inching their way along the congested northbound Pasadena Freeway and the eastbound 210 Freeway that led them back to the mall in Arcadia to retrieve her car. It was then that he put his arms around her and drew her closer to him. Neither one spoke, for there was a mutual understanding between the forgiving and the forgiven.

Emily followed her father home and by the time they arrived, she had gotten her emotions under control. Upon entering the house, fragrant with spicy cinnamon cider, her mother asked, "Where have you two been? I was beginning to worry."

"Oh, Emily called and we had to take care of some car trouble that took longer than we had planned," her husband grinned, winking at his daughter. "Now let's eat and get busy trimming that Christmas tree."

After dinner, Emily excused herself saying she had quite a bit of homework to do. As soon as she reached her room upstairs, she called Lakisha, apologizing profusely for her rotten behavior.

"Can you ever forgive me? And how did you get home? I completely forgot about leaving you stranded after the security guard dragged me away."

"Girl, you're not gonna believe this, but as I was leaving Macy's to catch a bus back to school, I ran into Mike and Ramón, who were also cutting class! We went for a snack and then I bummed a ride home off of them."

"So we're still good? I mean you've forgiven me?"

"Yeah. Lucky for you, we're not the only ones with senioritis. Just don't get any more bright ideas about stealing, okay?"

"I learned my lesson. No more risky behavior for me. It's just that I'm so ready to move on!"

"Most of us are, but from what I hear, by the time graduation rolls around, we'll be all weepy and teary-eyed, sad to leave high school. I guess we'd better make the most of our last few months."

"You're the best, Lakisha. Thanks for everything. Gotta go now and get started on my homework. It's gonna be a late-nighter for me because I'm getting such a late start."

Thus ended Emily's foray into the life of a shoplifter. What she really came to love and cherish about that fateful cold December night was the discovery of what a truly great man her father was and how blessed she was to have Lakisha as her best friend.

The Gift

———

Mrs. Nora Brown, a slender brunette in her late thirties, taught English at a junior high just south of San Francisco, California, where the kids came from less-than-affluent families. Many were living below the poverty level, others slightly above, while few could be considered from middle class or upper middle class homes. The kids were acutely aware that the San Francisco Bay Area was filled with more "haves," rather than "have-nots." They also knew that many cultural advantages abounded on the peninsula for those who could afford to partake of them.

School activities that necessitated expenditures beyond what the families could afford often left many of the adolescents on the outside looking in, so to speak. Those who were lucky enough to have older siblings were occasionally able to muster up suitable clothing for such events as winter formals and graduation dances. For many, the cost of field trips to places such as Fisherman's Wharf, Golden Gate Park, the de Young Museum and Japanese Tea Garden, and performances at the venerable Curran and Geary Theaters or the War Memorial Opera House were out of the question.

Nora Brown was ever sensitive to the plight of many of her students, so she always maintained a "slush fund" for those who could not incur the additional expenses that came with Associated Student Body (ASB) activities. She was also appreciative of the fact that the few students who did have discretionary dollars to spend did not flaunt their good fortune. Some even shared their allowances to cover a few modest financial needs of their peers, such as lunch and sundry school supplies.

Now Nora Brown, ever the staunch supporter of public schools, had several friends who taught in private schools. On a Saturday afternoon in December, she had a rare opportunity to lunch with two friends, Dorothy and Irene.

"Honestly, Nora, I don't understand why you bother with those public school kids and huge classes," Dorothy, her neighbor, chided her. "You really ought to look into working at one of the private schools in San Francisco or farther down the peninsula."

"Why would I want to do that?" asked the proud public school teacher. "I have nothing against private schools, but I love my work despite the challenges."

"Well, you know, kids are much better behaved and the curriculum is more rigorous in private schools," Irene responded, dabbing her lips on a white linen napkin. "They get a superior education and furthermore, the teachers are quite excellent."

"Oh, really?" retorted Nora Brown. "Did it ever occur to you that those who teach at private *and* public schools are all educated by the same instructors and professors from their institutions of higher learning?"

Silence ensued from the ladies. Nora Brown continued, "Let's say that forty would-be teachers are education majors at Stanford University. Twenty graduate and begin their careers in public schools and twenty are hired to teach at private schools. All forty of them sat in the same classes, heard identical lectures, and completed similar assignments. Are you saying that somehow being in a private school environment makes teachers smarter? More capable?"

"Okay, maybe not, but there are other perks in private schools," insisted Nancy. "Classes are smaller and you get those great ski vacations during the winter. Also, the kids give some fabulous gifts at Christmas time. Did I ever tell you all about the two tickets I got for a night at the opera last year? Fabulous!" exclaimed Nancy, "Simply fabulous!"

Nora Brown wasn't bothered because her friends thought it odd that she endured the rigors of public school teaching. After all, she didn't need the money. Her husband was a concert pianist who performed with many of the best orchestras throughout the country when he wasn't on tour giving solo recitals or playing in chamber music concerts. It had always been Nora's desire to teach ever since she could remember. She wasn't in it for the time off or gifts from her students. Yes, it would be nice to have smaller classes, but there was much she enjoyed about working with the underdogs and helping kids to pursue their passions. She had no regrets.

The conversation eventually drifted to other topics including the dreadful natural gas line explosion of 2010 in San Bruno, one of their favorite movies, *Moneyball,* depicting the Oakland Athletics baseball team, San José's fabulous Martin Luther King Jr. Library, the annoying thick fog that rolls in late each afternoon, nude bicycle riding events in San Francisco, and aren't they shocking annual events? After conversation had run its course and Nora Brown returned home, she faced an evening of paper grading. Why did she assign those essays so close to Christmas when she still had more shopping to do and that party to plan for some of their friends from the San Francisco Symphony?

The last day before winter break, students came with modest gifts for their friends and a sprinkling of presents for their teachers. Nora Brown always got a variety of homemade cards and notes with messages such as, "I'll try harder next semester, Mrs. B. Thanks for putting up with me. Try to have a nice Christmas anyway." Or, "Sorry I didn't do so well, but thanks for helping me after school." Or, "Merry Christmas to my favorite teacher. I hope I get a good grade in this class."

There was one frail boy with sandy brown hair and hazel eyes who lingered after the others had left the period just before lunch. He shyly approached his teacher and handed her a gift wrapped in the remnants of a brown paper bag. "It's all I could afford, Mrs. Brown, but I hope you like it."

"Oh, Johnny, if you made it, I know I'll like it."

She proceeded to open the gift and withdrew a plastic egg with a face drawn on it, attached to the handle of a small egg whip. Around the "neck" of the egg-person there was a blue and white checked ribbon fashioned in the style of a bow tie. He had cut up some yellow yarn for hair and pasted it on top of the egg's head.

"It's lovely, Johnny," she exclaimed as she moved closer to give him a hug. "I have the perfect place for it on my desk." She paused, studying the gift. "Shall we give him a name?"

"A name? Okay, sure." He thought a bit. "How about Edgar?"

"Done!" She shook the little egg-person gently and said, "Do you hear that? Your new name is Edgar." They both laughed.

"You really like it? It isn't much, but I made it just for you."

"This *is* a perfect gift because you made it for me and that's why it's so special. I shall think of you while sitting at my desk with Edgar." Johnny sheepishly gave her another hug and slipped out the door.

Nora Brown sat at her desk turning the diminutive egg-person round and round in her hands, transfixed by this home-spun creation from the heart. She thought of her friends who would be opening lavish store-bought gifts or tickets to who-knows-where from their well-to-do students, but she did not envy them. Nora Brown and her husband could buy their own opera tickets and pay for weekend trips, but she could never buy herself an egg-person with a blue and white checked bow tie. She also knew that her supportive husband would see the value of the gift. As a matter of fact, he would most likely want Edgar to spend some time with him at his piano where he proudly displayed numerous past offerings his wife's students had bestowed upon her.

Opera Boy

Giulio Benedetto was one hundred per cent Italian who resembled a younger version of actor Jonah Hill. Two stereotypical thoughts often come to mind regarding Italians: 1) They crave pasta. 2) They love opera. Giulio, true to his heritage, was enamored of both these things. Indeed, there were times when he overindulged in too much of his mother's superb cuisine and he carried some extra pounds as proof.

As for opera, well, it was his passion and in his blood. Giulio's inspiration came from the world's greatest tenors including the late Enrico Caruso, Mario Lanza, and Luciano Pavarotti, plus the still-active stars, Plácido Domingo, Jonas Kaufmann, James Courtney, and José Carreras, to name a few. He must have seen Mario Lanza's starring role in the 1950's movie, *The Great Caruso,* dozens of times. Not that he had anything against the pop and rock artists of the day, for he listened to them, too, and was an avid follower of TV's *American Idol*. However, his passion was opera.

What was on Giulio's iPod, you might ask? His favorite operas included Puccini's *Madama Butterfly* (based on the true story of a Japanese woman, Cio Cio San, who married an American Navy Lieutenant during WWII, only to be abandoned by him when he returns to Japan with his American wife whereupon Cio Cio San commits suicide in despair), Puccini's *Tosca* (about the fictionalized famous opera singer, Floria Tosca, who jumps to her death at the end of the opera after witnessing the execution of her lover ordered by the jealous Scarpia), *La Bohème* ("The Bohemians," centering on the lives of young struggling artisans in Paris, 1830), and Verdi's *La Traviata* ("The Lost One," dealing with the aftermath of a scandalous and ill-fated love affair between Violeta and Alfredo and their subsequent misunderstandings). This collection was certainly not the usual musical fare for a young boy's iPod.

Giulio loved the over-the-top drama, with the elaborate sets and costumes, and convoluted plots that demanded the audience suspend all sense of reality and willingly enter a world of mystery, passionate love, unspeakable violence, but above all, breath-takingly beautiful music. No doubt about it, opera coursed through his veins as did the blood that kept his body alive.

For all his love of this demanding art form requiring days of hourly practice, years of study, memorization, and vocal training, could Giulio sing? What about *his* voice? Oh, yes, this boy was born to sing, an Italian tenor to the core. With proper vocal coaching and the discipline to learn the tenor roles, there would be no stopping him.

He was in the tenth grade and had begun studying with an opera coach in the San Francisco Bay Area. He was willing to pay the price in terms of dedication, long hours of study, commutes from Richmond in the East Bay Area to San Francisco in the West Bay Area, and foregoing a "normal" adolescent life that would include football games, school dances, and hanging out with friends. These were easy sacrifices as far as he was concerned.

If he had his heart set on a career in opera, this was the time to begin the long road to performing in the finest opera houses in the world. He walked past one of the most famous among them each day on the way to his twice-weekly lessons: The War Memorial Opera House of San Francisco at 301 Van Ness Avenue, in the heart of the Civic Center. Occasionally, his teacher, Maestro Franco Gutierrez, who also coached many well-known singers from the San Francisco Opera Company, was able to procure some extra tickets for him and his parents. Oh, there was nothing better!

His loving parents were supportive and worked hard to pay for his expensive lessons in the city. Mr. Benedetto owned a successful restaurant and his mother, who had once trained to become a concert pianist, taught lessons in her studio in back of their home.

Though Giulio, an only child, had a happy family life, he was a self-absorbed adolescent impervious to the sacrifices his supportive parents made to give him every advantage in developing his talent in hopes of eventually warding off the competitors who would soon cross his path. The ultimate goal for any serious American aspiring to sing opera is admission to the Metropolitan Opera Company at Lincoln Center in New York City, but one has to compete for those openings and the competition is fierce.

One day during lunch in the cafeteria, his backpack stuffed with books and music fell off the table and the contents spilled onto the floor. Among them were a book of *Bel Canto* vocal exercises and a libretto (a book with the opera text for the music) for Verdi's opera, *La Traviata*. He hurried to cram the items into his backpack, but it was too late. The two thugs, Alex and Nicklaus, sitting at a nearby table snatched up the books before Giulio could stash them away.

"Hey you, fat boy, what's up with the foreign language stuff? You sing?"

"Yeah," Giulio mumbled. He knew he was doomed now that his secret was out. You see, the high school was filled with unsavory characters and thugs who ran amok each day after school looking for trouble. Alex grabbed the book of vocal exercises and loudly began mocking operatic singing. Giulio reached for the book, but Alex jerked it away.

"Let's hear you sing, you punk Opera Boy," Nicklaus sneered.

"Please let me have my books," Giulio begged.

"Not until you sing, Opera Boy," sang Alex in his mocking hi-pitched falsetto voice while brandishing the books over his head.

"Is there a problem here?" asked Mr. Petrovich, an advanced algebra teacher who approached the boys while Alex was making a fool of himself, now the object of everyone's attention.

"No, no problem here, Mr. P. We was just wantin' to hear the boy sing, that's all," said Nicklaus in a sickeningly sweet voice.

"Then why do you boys have Giulio's opera books? Seems to me like *you* should be the ones singing. Go ahead, boys, sing for us now that you have everyone's attention."

By now, all the kids were looking at the two bullies, waiting for them to sing. "Sing for us, sing for us!" they chanted.

Alex and Nicklaus stood red-faced and mute as if suddenly changed into stone.

"No songs for us today?" prodded Mr. Petrovich.

Silence.

"Well, then, if you're not going to entertain us, I suggest you give the boy his books back. You've succeeded in making fools of yourselves in front of everyone here, so that's enough action for today. Let's wrap it up guys and move it on out of here. In case you haven't noticed, this is where people come to eat, not to be bullied."

The two boys stood glaring at Mr. Petrovich, then at Giulio.

"Out!" the teacher ordered.

Giulio appreciated being rescued by Mr. Petrovich, but he knew the boys were not done with him. There would be hell to pay some time down the line. The miscreants slunk dejectedly out the door while giving menacing glances over their shoulders.

He did not mention the incident to his parents that night at dinner. Rather, he headed straight for his room, after putting away an extra helping of lasagna, to begin working on a draft for an English paper on *Julius Caesar*.

Unlike most kids, he felt quite at home with the complex Elizabethan English of Shakespeare's plays. After all, he had already sung in several foreign languages, so the Shakespearean poetry was met with eager anticipation. As a matter of fact, other students in his class listened with rapt attention as he read the part of Julius Caesar each day. Truth be known, his peers may have been a bit envious of the ease and beauty of his interpretation as he declaimed the rhyming couplets so effortlessly. Not surprisingly, his speaking voice was as beautiful and melodious as his singing voice.

Contrary to the treatment meted out by Alex and Nicklaus, Giulio was treated with admiration and respect in this class. It was one of the few places where he felt completely accepted by his peers. It didn't hurt that the girls were drawn to him and he was sometimes good naturedly called "The Shakespearean Chick Magnet." His teacher was overjoyed by the interest everyone took in the play because of this one boy who transformed it into something that even a room full of teenagers could appreciate as great literature worth reading.

Things proceeded as normal with school, voice lessons, and preparations for an upcoming recital to take place at the San Francisco Conservatory of Music on 50 Oak Street, a short distance from the Opera House. All participants were to meet for rehearsal at the Conservatory one Monday afternoon in February. Giulio got off the bus near the Opera House as usual and began walking toward the conservatory. Suddenly, he sensed he was being followed; there was no doubt in his mind that his two stalkers were Alex and Nicklaus.

Large beads of sweat popped from his temples and forehead as he hastened his pace toward the Opera House, his place of refuge. *If only I can make it there before the guys get to me*, he thought. He ran to the stage door on the north side of the building but it was locked.

Pounding frantically, he hollered the name of his voice teacher, "Mr. Gutierrez, Mr. Gutierrez, please open the door! Heeeelp meeeee! Help!" He didn't dare look over his shoulder to confirm what he already knew: The two crazed predators, with only the devil's work on their minds, were closing in on him. He ran around the building only to find every door locked. Then he remembered, this was a Monday and the Opera House was always dark on Mondays so there was no reason for anyone to be there. Besides, this happened to be a Presidents' Day holiday.

"Opera Boy, you can't hide. We've got you now," came Nicklaus' sing-song taunts.

"Please leave me alone, *please*! What did I ever do to you?"

"You made us look like idiots in the cafeteria when Mr. Petrovich came along," sneered Nicklaus. "Now you're gonna pay."

"No, *I* didn't make you look stupid, *you* did that all by yourselves. If you remember correctly, I was minding my own business when you guys took my books. How is that my fault?"

"Oooooooh, this boy's got a mouth on him, ain't he, Nicky?" snickered Alex."

"Yeah, fat Opera Boy don't know when to keep his pie hole shut."

"Wul, maybe we'll have to fix that, won't we, Nicky?" Both boys pulled out their knives and instinctively, Giulio covered his throat with his hands as they circled around him menacingly, swiping their thighs with the serrated blades of their knives.

"No use grabbin' yer neck, Opera Boy. These knives'll cut right through yer hands *and* yer neck. It don't matter to us one way or the other how we slice you up."

"H-here, go ahead and take my books; take my money, but just leave me alone," Giulio begged.

"We don't want yer books'r yer money. We wanna silence yer freakin' pie hole fer good. Got it, Opera Boy?" Alex bared his teeth and let out a death-defying cackle. He stepped back to take in the grandeur of the magnificent façade of the building that had come to mean so much to the doomed tenor. "Aw, ain't it sad, Opera Boy?" Alex continued while brushing the blade against Giulio's cheek. He grabbed a wad of his hair and spun him around. "Take a final look cuz this'll be the last time you'll ever think 'bout singin' that crap around here." They got on either side of him, forcing him to a more obscure location behind the trees at the north end of the building.

Nicklaus looked around nervously. "Yo! We better do our business and get the hell outa here. Keep an eye peeled, will ya?" Since it was a Presidents' Day holiday, the streets were unusually quiet and by now they were in the deep shadows of the trees. Without warning, Nicklaus jumped Giulio and threw him to the ground. They struggled while Alex looked on making sure no cops or adults were around. Nicklaus raised his knife and Giulio suddenly jerked his head aside just as the blade, meant for his throat, landed at the base of his hairline on the left side of his neck. Blood spurted everywhere from the deep jagged gash made by the serrated blade. With his one free hand, Giulio rammed two stiffened fingers straight into Nicklaus' left eye that resulted in a blood-curdling scream. When Alex rushed to his aid, Giulio made his getaway, half running, half staggering alternately toward the Conservatory, leaving his blinded blood-spattered adversary pawing the ground in agony.

By the time Giulio reached his destination, staggering now and holding his neck, he was covered in blood, completely impervious to the seriousness of his wound but looking ghastly pale. It was strictly the adrenaline rush along with his survival instincts that propelled him toward the Conservatory. When safely inside, he took a few steps whereupon he collapsed into the arms of Maestro Gutierrez who had run toward his injured student, just in time to catch him. The force of his fall caught them both off balance and as a result, they slumped to the ground.

Giulio's eyelids fluttered as he uttered faintly, "I'm so sorry, so sor —" Then he went slack.

"Oh, *oh*, dear *God*! He's been stabbed!" cried Maestro Gutierrez. "Martha, quick, call an ambulance down here. We need to get him up to St. Mary's Medical Center *now*!" The appalled staff member hurriedly phoned as instructed. Someone rushed over with a towel so the frantic musician could apply it to the gaping wound. The boy was in shock now and lay listlessly in his teacher's arms. "You will pull through this, I promise," he whispered, stroking the boy's dark matted hair, pulling his limp body closer. "Stay with us Giulio; don't leave us, I'm begging you. Don't leave us! Please, dear God, don't take him from us now. He has his whole life ahead of him. He's such a gift to us all." His tears fell on the boy's face, mingling with the blood splotches on his cheeks.

The other young musicians stood back looking on helplessly, some crying, others hugging one another. One of the boys could be heard whispering, "Thank God they didn't get his larynx. If he pulls through this, he'll still be able to sing and that's some comfort."

If he pulls through . . .

As the ambulance siren drew near, Maestro Gutierrez looked up at Martha again and asked, "Martha, will you please call Giulio's parents while I go to the hospital with him? I'll remain there until his parents arrive and until we know what the outcome will be. Meanwhile, everyone should proceed with the rehearsal as this is your only chance to do so before the recital." By now, he was covered in Giulio's blood and the unthinkable preyed on his mind: *I can feel his life ebbing away. His pulse is weakening.*

The paramedics were quick to gather the limp boy up from his teacher's arms and placed him on the gurney that they slid into the back of the ambulance while Maestro Gutierrez climbed in behind. He sang softly to the failing boy while stroking his forehead, hoping in quiet desperation that somehow the music would sustain him.

It did not.

By the time they got Giulio into the operating room, his heart had flat lined. The would-be tenor with a brilliant operatic career in front of him was no more. His death could not have been more "operatic," in that it mirrored many of the tragedies in the works he so dearly loved. Maestro Gutierrez put his head down on the boy's arm and sobbed inconsolably. By the time Mr. and Mrs. Benedetto arrived, it was too late for them to see their son alive.

The distraught maestro and mentor left the grieving parents alone to mourn the death of their son while he remained in a private waiting room until the Benedettos joined him. The three sat crying, huddled together, still having no idea how and where the attack took place or who his attackers were.

If there was one shard of light that could be shed on the tragic loss of a young, gifted teenager, it was this: When Giulio made his way to the conservatory, he left a trail of blood that led police from the place of attack. He also literally fingered his attacker by poking him in the eye, doing considerable damage in a desperate act of self-defense. As Nicklaus lay writhing on the ground with Alex hovering over him, a passerby noticed the two boys near the trees and became suspicious when she spotted the bloody knife that somehow ended up on the sidewalk. Upon seeing the boy's weapon, she casually walked to the south end of the building and ducked behind the trees there to dial 911.

The police called for an ambulance to take Nicklaus to the hospital for treatment of his now-sightless eye and Alex was taken into custody. Backup officers were called to follow the trail of blood that led them to the Conservatory. Martha filled the officers in on what transpired, indicating that Giulio had been taken to St. Mary's Medical Center, accompanied by Maestro Gutierrez. Thus, by putting together all the pieces of the puzzle, and by sharing their information with the Benedettos and Maestro Gutierrez at the hospital, they were able to determine that this was a homicide.

Every student in Giulio's English class came to his memorial service held at the magnificent Grace Cathedral, high atop Nob Hill. In a special tribute to him and his love for Shakespeare, students, along with their teacher, read from a book of his sonnets. Fellow musicians from the Conservatory sang some of his favorite opera arias and duets. They had just performed the recital, dedicated to their fallen friend, so there was an abundance of beautifully-performed music to be heard.

Had Giulio mentioned anything about potential trouble with the two boys who had mocked him in the cafeteria, things may have turned out differently. However, by targeting the most vulnerable part of his attacker's face, he inadvertently identified his murderer and may have spared others who were "different" from a similar fate.

What better way to end this sad story than with a quote from the great Italian tenor, Luciano Pavarotti (1935-2007)? "Above all, I am an opera singer. This is how people will remember me," and with Shakespeare's flawed hero, King Lear, who lamented, "I am more sinned against than sinning."

Celebrities as Stomach

———

There are some unusual children who defy explanation. Most want to fit in with their peers, but what about those who don't? Do they become "different" by choice or have environmental circumstances set them apart from their peers without them realizing they stand out as odd, different, or at least, a bit unusual?

Mike Harrison was one such boy. He was shy, obedient, and a B-C student in the ninth grade. He didn't look different from his peers, but there was one distinct oddity about the child: He saw people as stomach-shaped entities and drew them as such. He created an entire sketchbook filled with drawings entitled, "Abraham Lincoln as Stomach," "Judge Joe Brown as Stomach," "Hank Aaron as Stomach," "Ray Charles as Stomach," "George Washington as Stomach," and so on.

It was clear to Miss O'Reilly that Mike was not inspired by the likes of Flemish masters of the past who strove for photographic realism, or the French Impressionists who created blurred renderings of their subjects as if seen from a moving train. No, Mike's mentors were the abstract artists such as Cubist painter, Pablo Picasso, and the Dutch lithographer and graphic artist, M.C. Escher, famous for creating optical illusions.

One day, his teacher, Miss O'Reilly, stopped by his desk and asked to see his work. "Mike, let's see what you've done today on your history assignment."

He looked up shyly, "Um, I haven't finished the notes yet, but here's what I do have." When he handed her his work, she noticed the sketches. "Jennifer Lopez as Stomach?" she asked, raising an eyebrow. "What's this all about?" He quickly covered the drawing with his hands.

A few students sitting around him began to snicker. "Yeah, he always draws those silly pictures," one girl commented derisively. "He's weird."

Miss O'Reilly could see that she had created a vulnerable situation for the boy, so after reprimanding the girl for her rude remarks, she quickly moved away from Mike's desk and engaged the class in another activity.

For the next few days, Miss O'Reilly couldn't get Mike and his drawings out of her mind. She asked him to stay after class one day to get a closer look at his sketches and perhaps determine the cause of Mike's fascination with the stomach.

"I'm working on a whole new series about a current court case on television," he announced proudly as he presented her with his sketchpad. She looked through each page and was dumbfounded not only by what a splendid artist he was, but also by how creatively he worked each subject into the shape of a stomach.

"So Mike, what's the connection between the stomach and your subjects? Why not draw simple portraits of these people?" she wanted to know.

"Well, I have no fascination with the shape of the stomach, but the point is this: Anyone can draw regular portraits of people as people. Where's the creativity in that?"

She couldn't argue with his logic. He had skillfully clothed his subjects as they appeared in real life, transformed by their stomach-shaped torsos. The faces of his subjects were brilliantly executed to the exact likeness of the real life celebrities, some living, others dead. He was not just a gifted artist; his work had an M. C. Escher magic about it.

"These are truly brilliant, Mike, and utterly charming. How do you think this stuff up?"

"Glad you like them." He smiled, then paused, looking down dejectedly at his work spread out on Miss O'Reilly's desk.

"Why the long face, Mike? These are really good. It's so wonderful to see kids with great imaginations like this. You should be proud of your gift."

"Well, it's hard being different. People make fun of me and call me 'Stomach Boy.' Why can't they just accept who I am and leave me alone?"

"Hmmmmm. I suspect there are a couple of things going on here. First, it doesn't take a rocket scientist to see what a gifted artist you are. Most likely, many kids are jealous of your talent. They would like to draw as well as you but they can't. Also, people often fear what they don't understand or what seems out of the ordinary to them. Depicting the celebrities as stomach-shaped beings is way out of their realm of thought."

"You really think I have talent?"

"I *know* you do." She paused as an idea occurred to her. "Here's a plan, if you're interested: We'll put up some of your best drawings so kids will get used to seeing them. I draw well, too, so I'll post some of my Celebrities as Stomach along with yours. Make sure you sign yours and I'll sign mine. If they see enough of these, they won't seem so strange any more. She paused again to assess his mood. "Are you in?"

"I'm in!" he smiled. "You really think this will work?"

"Well, it would be a bit awkward for them to criticize your work when mine is hanging beside it. I can't wait to see their faces when they view our joint collection of drawings on display, say by next Monday?"

"Okay, I'll have some ready by then."

Later in the week, another boy – a bit on the chubby side with black curly hair – came by Miss O'Reilly's room after school and asked if some of his artwork could be displayed as well. "Mike told me you are going to hang some of his work next week. He made me promise not to tell the other kids. I wouldn't do that because I'm his best friend."

She was relieved to know he had at least one good friend in this boy, Duron. "Here's the deal I'll cut with you. Do you draw well?"

"Yes, I'm pretty good."

"Then would you be willing to draw and sign some Celebrities as Stomach pieces to fill out the collection Mike and I are making?"

"Awesome! Yeah, I'll do it! You doin' it too, Miss O?"

"Yes, I've put together several of them for Monday's showing. Just make sure you and Mike are here early so we can put them up before first period."

"Oh, man! This is going to be so much fun! I promise I won't tell anyone." He made a zip motion across his lips and vanished out the door.

As agreed, the two boys arrived early Monday morning so they could post the drawings. When the first period students entered, a hush fell over the class. It was the first time Miss O'Reilly "heard" complete silence from all thirty-six students who stood huddled before the abstract drawings with their mouths agape. Seen individually, they thought the drawings were strange and that Mike was nothing short of a bizarre freak for creating them. However, when they beheld the entire collection on all four walls, it had a stunning impact upon them. They remained speechless, in awe.

In a hushed whisper, a girl finally asked, "Duron, you draw these, too?"

"Yeah, they're fun to make."

Another student, "And you, too, Miss O'Reilly?"

"Me, too," she smiled. As she hoped, her little scheme had succeeded brilliantly and she looked with pride upon her students who stood in awe before the display.

In a matter of days, students from all of Miss O'Reilly's classes were busy drawing Celebrities as Stomach. It was now the cool thing to do. If you couldn't draw a Celebrity as Stomach, well, you were simply out of it. By the end of the month, the classroom walls were covered with living and dearly departed celebrities. To her credit, Miss O'Reilly had succeeded in normalizing the behavior of her students; Mike's drawings no longer seemed odd to them.

A couple of weeks later, annual parent conferences were being held in the cafeteria during a three-day period. The last day of conferences fell on Halloween. Mike was sitting with Duron at Miss O'Reilly's table waiting for his mother to join them. Their backs were to the entranceway. While they sat chatting, in came a woman, nothing short of an apocalyptic vision, wandering up and down the aisles among the tables.

Her long, stringy hair had been dyed several different colors – or was it a wig? – and she was clothed in a tattered sleeveless pink nightgown, shuffling along in her faded pink bedroom slippers. A hush fell over the cafeteria as students, parents, and teachers paused to view what surely had to have been someone in a Halloween costume.

However, after wandering seemingly without purpose, it became apparent to all that she was no joke. There was a disturbed person in their midst, so who would make the first move to intercede on her behalf?

Mike turned to see why everyone was so quiet all of a sudden. Then he saw her. Without hesitation, he rose from the bench and went over to the disoriented woman. Greeting her with a hug, and with dignity and poise rarely seen in one so young, he took her by the hand and led her over to Miss O'Reilly's table.

"Miss O'Reilly, I'd like you to meet my mom, Mrs. Harrison. She came here for the conference." The silence that continued among those inhabiting the cafeteria could only be interpreted as a metaphor for the admiration and pity everyone must have felt for Mike as peer, student, and son. As for Miss O'Reilly, the conference was a blur. She was aware of the strong stench of alcohol and cigarettes surrounding the woman and she felt certain that any comments made about her gifted son went unperceived.

Why are some children different?

A contributing factor in Mike's case may have had something to do with being raised by an alcoholic parent. No matter the reason. It all comes down to our perception of what it means to be different. Once we get used to the differences, they become the new norms. Whatever happened to be the perceptions of "different" and "normal" that Halloween day, Miss O'Reilly was sure of one thing: Mike was the mentor of everyone in the room, for all looked upon him with awe and admiration, just as students had done a couple of weeks earlier when gazing upon his unique artistic talent.

The Little Class That Could

"Group think" is a term that applies to students who share the same impression of themselves in a class: We are too smart to listen to what you (the teacher) have to say. We know everything already. We learned that last year, so we can coast this year. We are too dumb to learn this stuff. We'll never succeed, so why try? So we fail. Big whoop.

Mr. Peterson, a strapping six-foot-three African American teacher in his early thirties had a situation in his ninth grade English class. From the first day they entered his room, it was apparent all were entering with the attitude they were doomed to failure. Their body language spoke volumes. They might just as well have been wearing hair shirts to punish themselves for their self-inflicted stupidity.

Mr. Peterson wasted no time in addressing their demeanor. "My goodness, look at yourselves. Here you are with your whole lives ahead of you and you look like you've been sentenced to be buried alive on some deserted island."

No response came from the listless kids staring straight ahead, arms folded tightly across their chests. They were a dull-eyed humorless lot.

Mr. Peterson walked slowly up and down the aisles, studying them, becoming absorbed in their silence. *Good grief,* he thought, *these kids are really hurting. Looks like I have my work cut out for me.*

Without saying a word, he went to the Promethean Board (a computerized white board) and wrote: *You have ten minutes to write one or two paragraphs describing where you see yourself after high school. You need not put your name on the paper, but everyone must complete the assignment.* His strategy was to meet silence with silence.

There were a few low groans and a bit of eye rolling, but still nobody spoke. Mr. Peterson roamed the room, monitoring the students as they worked. When he was satisfied that everyone had finished, again he went to the white board and wrote: *Now write one or two paragraphs about what you'd <u>like</u> to be doing after high school.*

Again, he traveled the room, keeping an eye on them. When it appeared they had finished, he gave one last instruction on the board: *Describe what you think might prevent you from accomplishing what you'd <u>like</u> to be doing after high school.*

When they had finished, he collected their work, shuffled all the papers, and redistributed them to the class. Finally, he spoke: "Now, read the paper that has been given to you while I wait." They eyed him quizzically, but dutifully started reading papers from their unnamed peers.

Now, a different kind of quiet fell over the class. The "new silence" was one of complete engagement, utter absorption. Mr. Peterson knew what they were thinking without ever reading their papers. This was a remedial English class of students who had been grouped in a low-level track. It was their lot to endure the stigma of Remedial English on their program cards. This was not a class of foreign-born students; these were kids born and raised in the USA who somehow had fallen through the cracks.

The very purpose of Mr. Peterson's assignment was to enable the students to see that they were not alone. They were all in this together. Their newly-acquired revelation would serve as the starting point for this small class of frustrated students.

"What if I told you this could become a regular English class?"

"No way," came a voice from the back. "We've been stupid all our lives."

"Stupid, or undereducated?" asked Mr. Peterson. The class stared blankly at him. He stared back. "Well? Which is it? I'm waiting for an answer."

"I want to know what do you mean by *undereducated*?" The same voice from the back wanted to know.

"I mean, do you see yourselves as underachievers because you *can't* learn or because you *won't* learn?"

"Never thought of it that way before," spoke a girl from the front.

"If that sentiment applies to all of you, allow me to adjust your thinking about yourselves. Let's start with the basics: You found your way to class, didn't you?" Heads nodded. "You followed directions and wrote the assignment, did you not?" Again, heads nodded. "Finally, you read and understood each other's papers, did you not?"

Silence.

"Is there anyone here who could not perform those tasks?" No hands went up, so Mr. Peterson took that as a "no." He paused, eyeing his class, then continued, "Here's some breaking news: Stupid people could not have completed those tasks."

"Wul, why are we in this stupid class then?" came another query from a sultry blonde twisting a strand of hair around her forefinger.

"The word is 'well,' not 'wul.' Our attitude adjustment will begin by speaking correctly, so lose the dumb and dumber talk. If you act stupid or speak stupidly, people will treat you as such. Do I make myself clear?" The eyes of this normally good-natured man turned to a cold, steely brown. He hated to see kids demean themselves with what he called "idiot speech" so often acclaimed by the movie industry that often depicts teens displaying moronic behavior.

The girl nodded, head bowed, while shifting uncomfortably in her chair.

"You are all in this class because you made bad choices. You're not stupid; you're undereducated *by choice*. Nobody put a gun to your heads forcing you not to do assignments, not to study for tests, not to attend class, or not to seek help when needed. These are all choices and I'll bet these were made by every one of you along the way. Am I right?"

Heads nodded sheepishly.

Eyes rolled.

"Brace yourselves because tomorrow will mark a major turning point in your undereducated lives. We'll call it The End-of-Bad-Choices Day." He glanced up at the clock. "It's time to clean up, so remain seated until the bell rings and wait until I dismiss you."

The following day, the students looked a bit more alive as they entered Mr. Peterson's classroom. Not that there was a spring to their step or a song in their hearts, but at least the looks of defiance and despair had lessened somewhat. Mr. Peterson stood at the door greeting everyone upon entering.

When they were in their places, all sat facing the Promethean Board over which sprawled a huge green and yellow banner displaying the mantra, TODAY IS END-OF-BAD-CHOICES DAY.

He waited for the message to boot up in their brains. Then he spoke smiling, "Good morning, everybody. As promised yesterday, we're putting an end to bad choices. From now on, each of you will be responsible for each other's success. It's called *peer pressure*. This is not a new term for you. You've heard it used in connection with negative actions: bullying, drugs, ditching class, or criminal behavior. However, in here, *peer pressure* will take on a whole new meaning. We're going to apply it in a positive sense. Your grades will be posted daily, so everyone will know who the slackers and achievers are. The achievers will sit with the slackers on teams with a mixture of both. The goal, of course, is to eventually have each team comprised solely of achievers."

"Wul – er – Well, how can we be responsible for someone else's failures? That hardly seems fair."

"Life isn't fair. Many of you already know that from your personal experiences. However, that's no excuse. You will be responsible for each other because you will learn to care about the individuals in this class. If the slackers succeed, you all will succeed. Our class goal is a minimum 3.00 GPA."

"You're joking!"

"No way!"

"Impossible."

"My highest grade in English was a D."

He let them have their say. Then he pointed to the sign, reminding them that bad choices were no longer allowed. "You will achieve a class GPA of no less than 3.00 if you make that *choice*. You will learn to care because your success will depend on others' success. How will that happen you might ask?"

A student whose hand was raised slowly lowered it as Mr. Peterson continued.

"Here's how: To begin with, some of your tests and written assignments will be given a 'class grade.' Points on particular assignments will be totaled and averaged into one number so you'll all receive the same grade on that assignment.

"So if John gets an F and Maria gets an A, they both get a C? That hardly seems fair."

"See? You've already proven you're not stupid," smiled Mr. Peterson. "You get it. You understand the concept. John will get an F only if his teammates allow him to slide by without doing the work. If that happens, Maria will indeed lose her A."

"How do we know what teams we're on?"

"When I correct the first assignment, the grades will be posted. Then the low and high achievers will be paired up. In other words, the teams will be created from grade results."

"Will you grade on the curve – on the top student's grade?" The voice sounded so pathetically hopeful, Mr. Peterson wanted to laugh, but he maintained his composure.

"Oh, no. We start from the number of points possible." He wrote *criterion reference grading* on the board and compared the difference between the two grading systems. The students' eyes widened.

The "D" student began, "But other teachers grade on a curve and –"

"And how has that been working for you? You just said your highest grade in English was a D, which leads me to believe your others were Fs, correct?"

With head bowed, he nodded in agreement.

"Then I rest my case," affirmed Mr. Peterson, pointing to the bulleted list on the board. He continued, "So then, here's a summary of procedures written on the board:

- All grades will be posted.

- Teams will consist of slackers and achievers until all become achievers.

- You are responsible for each other's academic well being.

- Grade scales will be based on the total number of possible points, never on a curve.

- Your personal success will depend on the achievements of everyone in this room.

- Our long-term goal is a class GPA of no less than a 3.00.

- You will take responsibility for your own education.

- You will be held accountable for making up any work missed from absences or tardies.

- Two tardies will result in a call home and detention to be held after school with me."

He paused, surveying his stunned students who by now looked like they had been changed into blocks of wood.

"Any questions?" he asked.

They sat numbed and stone-faced, knowing they were trapped in Mr. Peterson's English Boot Camp. They felt resentment for being coerced and subjected to his winner-takes-all approach, but they also secretly appreciated that somebody cared enough about them to set firm boundaries, accepting no option other than success.

As the class exited, filing past Mr. Peterson standing at the door, he overheard one of the students whisper, "He actually believes we can pull this off. I guess it's worth a shot." Mr. Peterson smiled. This wasn't his first boot camp class and it wouldn't be his last. He knew what lay ahead and he relished the challenge. He had three young children of his own and hoped that their new teachers were being as tough on them as he was with his ninth graders.

In the early stages of English Boot Camp, there was much verbal sniping among the students. The slackers were resentful of the achievers for always "being up in my grill" or "on my case." The achievers were exasperated by the lack of effort exhibited by the slackers. "Díos mío, Mr. Peterson!" exclaimed Miguel. "What ever made you want to become a teacher? It's impossible getting some of these kids to work. It shouldn't be our responsibility. This really sucks," he whined.

"Oh, but we *should* be responsible for one another's well being when it comes to striving for excellence. Helping one another is the best way you can move beyond the boundaries of a remedial English class. It's a good way to get your collective brains fired up," he smiled.

As the weeks pressed on, however, the mood gradually shifted. Either the slackers tired of the achievers being "in my business and up in my grill" or they genuinely began to enjoy experiencing success. The achievers grew less anxious because they could see the improvement made by their under-achieving peers.

One day, Mr. Peterson put a new task to them: "I'm passing out the grade sheets with all the teams' work to date. We are four months into boot camp now and I want each team to calculate the number of members who are in in the C-A grade range and those who are still earning Ds and Fs. Let me know what you've discovered by the end of the period. One reporter from each team will state the number of slackers and achievers on his/her team. You do not have to give names. Just state the number in each category."

"Do you know the team results, Mr. Peterson?" asked a slacker-turned-achiever.

"Indeed I do. Let's see how good you are in math. This is a little cross-curricular exercise," he smiled. He monitored the teams busying themselves with their calculations.

When each group had finished, he numbered them from one to seven. "Okay, time's up. We will proceed in numerical order with your reports. Team One, what were your findings?"

"We have three achievers and only one slacker," came the proud response from the reporter for Team One.

"Team Two?" said Mr. Peterson.

"Still two slackers – but they're almost achieving – and two achievers."

"Team Three?"

"Four achievers." A unanimous cheer went up from the class.

"Team Four?"

"One slacker, three achievers."

"Team Five?"

"Three slackers and only one achiever. Emily and Denzel hardly ever come to school, so we're being penalized by their absences."

"Okay, I'll call home again," said Mr. Peterson. "Maybe we'll have to set up a Student Study Team with their parents and teachers. If they remain 'no-shows,' we'll take them out of the GPA mix." A sigh of relief went up among the students. "Let's continue. Team Six?"

"Four achievers." More cheers came from the class.

"And finally, Team Seven?"

"Four, count them, *four* achievers," boasted the eager team representative.

Mr. Peterson smiled at his happy class that had come alive over the past few months. When their high-fiving and self-congratulatory cheering subsided, he spoke.

"Last September, you entered this room convinced you were all too stupid to achieve. Most of you were slackers, convinced you would never meet the 3.00 GPA goal. Now we have only seven students who still need to get their act together. Twenty-one of you are achievers. How does that feel?"

They smiled back at him. As if planned in advance, several students asked at once, "May we spend the rest of the period helping the others catch up so we can have one hundred per cent achievers?"

"Be my guest," Mr. Peterson obliged. "I'll just step aside and let you all figure this out." From that point on, he knew the others who still needed improvement would not let the class down. As promised, everyone *did* grow to care about each other. The more success they experienced, the more they wanted. Achievement became their drug of choice. Their teacher offered no extrinsic recompense or material incentive for their achievements; their reward would be strictly intrinsic, the simple knowledge that they were capable learners because somebody believed in them.

By the end of the year, Emily and Denzel had dropped out of school, perhaps moving to another district. As for the others, all seven teams had become achievers who contributed to the overall GPA of 3.40. When Mr. Peterson made the announcement the last week of school, they were beside themselves with joy. A unanimous cheer erupted from the class, "We're Number One! We're Number One!"

As for Mr. Peterson, he proudly looked upon his celebrating charges cheering and high-fiving one another. His was a special lead-from-behind, compassionate brand of low-profile inspiration. He was born to turn kids around and to bring out the best in them. As was his custom, he eagerly awaited the new challenges that lay ahead the following year in his Ninth Grade English Boot Camp.

Summer School

Russell Evans, a high school English teacher in his mid-fifties, always looked forward to teaching enrichment classes during summer school. Kids enrolled in these English classes because they loved literature and writing. This was during a time when school districts could afford enrichment courses as well as classes for students who needed to make up the subjects they failed during the school year.

This summer, however, brought him an odd collection of young people. There was Sammy who dropped out half way through summer school because he was arrested on a grand larceny charge.

Donny Wu came sporting ear labrets (pronounced LAY-brets), a custom made popular among some African tribe members who insert circular plates into their upper and lower lips and ear lobes. As the skin stretches, the plates are replaced with increasingly larger ones. Among some tribe members, it is not uncommon to see ear lobes and lips extended up to twelve inches or more in diameter. Donny's ear lobes now hung nearly to his shoulders.

Vivian was kicked out of her house because her alcoholic parents detested her boyfriend. She would rather lose the roof over her head than part with her companion covered with tattoos and body piercings, not to mention a couple of ear labrets. In short, he was all pierced and tatted up. Even through their alcoholic stupor, her parents couldn't embrace this match between their daughter and a mobile work of modern art otherwise known as Manuel.

Lamar and Annemarie sat in class on Friday of the second week sipping contents from their pint-sized thermos bottles. Mr. Evans noticed how their behavior grew increasingly bizarre and when called upon to read aloud, Lamar's speech was slurred. To confirm his suspicions, he asked Annemarie to read a passage aloud. Her speech was no better. As Mr. Evans suspected, the two of them were drunk! They had been imbibing Vodka from their thermoses, growing more intoxicated throughout the period. Needless to say, that was their grand finale to summer school.

Martin Balakian stole a P.E. teacher's wallet not realizing a security guard had been watching him. When confronted, he handed over the wallet, was booked by the police and taken away in handcuffs. Thus ended *his* summer school adventure.

By the end of the third week, Mr. Evans' class of thirty-five had dwindled to a mere twenty-four with the loss of the four aforementioned kids plus another seven miscreants. The saddest case, however, was Sonya Johansen, a petite strawberry blonde with freckles and green eyes. Her attendance had been sporadic, but when present, her work was of acceptable quality. However, something didn't seem right with her. She would ask to use the bathroom a couple of times each period and her clothes were increasingly loose but not baggy.

Mr. Evans knew something was wrong but he couldn't put his finger on the problem. She continued to produce acceptable work, behavior was fine, but he remained puzzled about her general appearance and frequent requests to leave the room.

Then by the end of the fifth week, he received a note from the office saying that Sonya Peterson would miss the last week because she was withdrawing from summer school. She was pregnant!

Oh, now I get it, he thought. *She kept leaving class because she had morning sickness. That also explains the larger ill-fitting clothes. Poor thing!*

In Sonya's desperate attempt to get help from the one teacher she thought could assist her, she called Mr. Evans at home in the middle of the last week of summer school.

"How did you get my number?" Mr. Evans wanted to know.

"The office gave it to me."

"So what's going on with you?"

"Hey, Mr. Evans, you gotta help me, *please.*"

"Help you with what, Sonya?"

"I can't have this baby! You *gotta* help me. If my sister finds out, she'll kick me out of her house."

"You live with your sister?"

"Yes, Mom kicked me out because I kept getting in trouble, so my sister took me in."

"What do you want me to do? Talk to your sister? Your mother?"

"Noooooo. I need an *abortion! I can't have this baby!"* Sonya wailed.

Mr. Evans was speechless. Of all the bizarre requests students had made in the past, this truly was the most stupefying.

"Hello? Are you still there?" asked the still-crying girl.

"Yes, I'm still here. You have left me speechless. How did you ever summon the nerve to ask a teacher to help you get an abortion? I'm completely stunned. What were you thinking?"

"Pleeeeeease help meeeee," she wailed. "I can't have this baby!"

"Sonya, I can't possibly help you with this request. What you're asking me to do is illegal not only because you're a minor, but also because you'll need the consent of your parent or legal guardian. I am neither of those. Do you even know how far along you have to be in your pregnancy before you *can't* have an abortion? I sure don't."

"No, I don't know. Oh, God! My sister will kill me!"

"You should have thought of that before getting pregnant. Don't you kids know anything about contraception?"

"What should I do *now*?" she asked, ignoring his question.

"There's no substitute for the truth. You'll have to tell your sister and your boyfriend; this is his problem, too. I seriously doubt your sister will kick you out. If she was compassionate enough to take you in when your mom turned her back on you, she won't turn on you now. Come September, you can attend the continuation high school while pregnant or even with the baby if you decide not to get an abortion.

"For real? I can still go to school?" Her voice sounded less desperate, more hopeful.

"Yes, and in addition to the regular subjects, you'll receive valuable instruction in prenatal care. Childcare is also provided for those who choose to keep their babies."

"You mean I can come to class with my baby? There are babies in the classroom?" she asked incredulously.

"Absolutely. When you calm down, you'll realize that whatever your decision, this is not the worst thing that could happen to you at this point. If you have the baby and put it up for adoption, you may possibly spend the rest of your life wondering what became of your child, but at least you will know that by so doing, you will have bestowed the gift of life on two deserving parents who are in a better position than you to raise a child. Whatever your choice, that will have to be your decision."

"Well, thanks for talking some sense into me. Things don't look so bad now. You think my sister will wig out when I tell her?"

"Oh, she'll be angry all right, you can count on that. You've taken advantage of her generosity and put her in a rather vulnerable position. You would be wise to keep quiet when she expresses her anger. Just let her vent. She'll eventually come around and help you get through this."

"Thanks a lot, Mr. Evans. I really appreciate your help and advice. Sorry to have bothered you, but I didn't know where else to turn."

"Right now you need a doctor not a teacher, so you'd better get a physical exam. Good luck with your decision and when school starts in the fall, drop by some time and let me know how you're doing."

"I will. Thanks."

Mr. Evans felt as though he had just dodged a bullet. In all his years of teaching, this had to be the most bizarre conversation with a student. As he was heading out to play a round of golf and clear his head, his wife entered the kitchen carrying a bag of groceries.

"Need any help carrying things in?" he asked.

"No thanks, I'm good. It looks like you're headed for the golf course. While you're out, I'm going to sit by the pool and read. Hope you score a 72 or lower," she smiled.

"Thanks. I'll be back in a couple of hours. Honey, you simply won't believe my latest summer school tale. Make sure you're sitting down when I tell you later."

He patted her lovingly on the cheek and vanished out the door, thankful that in some way he was able to help a troubled teen. Having had his curiosity piqued, he couldn't help wondering what her decision would be. *Guess I'll just have to wait until September to find out,* he thought while loading his golf clubs into the trunk of his car.

I Am Somebody!

Who would've thought a boy living with his father would need a mother? Certainly not the boy's mother. Dexter Hamilton was in the seventh grade and if ever there were a whirlwind of trouble, Dexter was it. He had black hair, pale skin, freckles and slightly protruding upper front teeth.

He was a neglected child of divorced parents who was at a loss to find his self-worth. It wasn't that the father physically mistreated his son; he simply didn't have time for him. There were none of the bonding activities so commonplace among father-son relationships where life progressed smoothly within a loving and stable family structure.

His mother "disappeared" shortly after the divorce and maintained minimal contact with her son thereafter. This didn't set well with Dexter and he was not about to be ignored by either parent any longer. He grew weary of kids asking, "Hey! Where's yo' mama!" or "You ain't got no mama? You musta been hatched by the stork!" "Why yo' mama don't love you?"

The cruel comments were unending and because Dexter was small for his age, he didn't feel secure enough to "bust some-one's chops" when kids taunted him. He would find another way to get noticed by his parents, even if it meant drawing negative attention to himself so they would *have* to come to the school and straighten out the problem. In short, Dexter was the perfect example of an old saying that no children will go unnoticed when their basic needs for love and respect are not met.

He first set his plan in motion by refusing to do any work. *Perfect,* he thought. *If I fail all classes, my mom will have to come to school and talk to my teachers.*

Thus began Operation Fail. Dexter stopped working, never studied for tests, and eventually succeeded in failing all his classes by the end of fall semester. Teachers spoke with him about his attitude and failing grades, as did his counselor. Did this get his parents' attention? No, it did not. There was no response from home, even when teachers tried to phone or e-mail.

All right, then, he reasoned. *Guess I'll have to ramp up Operation Fail.*

From then on, he did whatever he could to disrupt the class, drive the teacher nuts, and further alienate his peers. In short, he became the student from hell. Kids no longer laughed at his antics and teachers were at their wits' end. Eventually, he was kicked out of class so often he spent most of his school days in the office.

His next plan was a brilliant one, for at last he got his mother's attention. He began using his cell phone in class. This, of course, was against the school discipline code. When he pulled it out a second time in Mr. Martin's class, he warned the boy, "If I see that phone again, you will have to put it in my cupboard until a parent comes and picks it up or calls to have it returned to you."

Dexter dutifully did as instructed, and refrained from using the phone in class, only because he had a more sinister plan in mind. A couple of weeks later, he went to the vice principal and reported that his phone had been taken by Mr. Martin and when he went to get it out of the cupboard, it was missing.

Mr. Willows, the vice principal, called up Dexter's mother and asked her to come in and discuss the matter. "I'll come only if you have a police officer present," she insisted. "The very idea of a teacher stealing a child's cell phone is outrageous! What kind of school do you run, anyway?"

"Let's not jump to conclusions, Mrs. Hamilton. We can have a police officer present, but if the boy is lying about the phone, your demand will backfire and he'll be cited by the presiding officer."

"Fine," she agreed. "I know my boy wouldn't lie about such a thing."

Now Mr. Martin knew nothing of this exchange between Mr. Willows and Dexter's mother. The following day, he was grading papers after school when the phone rang. Mr. Willows was on the line.

"Mr. Martin, can you come down to my office now?" The nature of the request was not disclosed so Mr. Marin was surprised to be greeted by a "tribunal" consisting of the mother, the boy, a police officer, and the vice principal.

"What's going on here?" he wanted to know.

"You stole my cell phone," the boy blurted out.

"I did what?"

"You stole it. My phone. You stole it."

"No, Dexter, I did not even touch your phone. I simply asked you to put it away or I'd have you put it in the cabinet that I keep locked until a parent could come get it or call and ask that it be returned." He turned to the police officer, holding up the keys to his classroom. "Please, be my guest; you can go search Room 121. I was not informed in advance of this meeting, so I wouldn't have had the time or inclination to hide the phone. You can even check my briefcase, for I've nothing to hide."

"That won't be necessary. I get what's going on," responded the embarrassed officer, shifting uncomfortably in his chair. He looked at the vice principal, "You didn't tell Mr. Martin this meeting was scheduled with the boy and his mother?"

Mr. Willows looked a little sheepish. "No, I completely forgot. Things got so busy around here I neglected to tell Mr. Martin."

"So there was no input from you, Mr. Martin, before this meeting was called?" asked the officer.

"This is the first I knew of it when I walked in here."

"What seems to be the problem, Mrs. Hamilton?" the officer asked, looking directly at the boy's mother.

"If I may interrupt, I have a good idea of what the problem is," responded Mr. Martin. "Mrs. Hamilton, how long has it been since you've seen your son?"

"Let me think . . . about ten months."

"So during your absence, Dexter has failed all of his classes, he's been in trouble constantly with the school, and now you are finally motivated to come here and inquire about a cell phone?" he asked incredulously.

"Well, Dexter said you stole it and I believed him," she answered lamely.

"Did it occur to you that Dexter has been acting out because he is desperate to get your attention? It just seems odd that you've been absent from his life for ten months, yet you're concerned about a cell phone that he most likely still has in his possession."

"Well, they're not cheap and I didn't want to replace it."

"I'm sad that no one has spoken about Dexter's anger, hurt, and lack of academic achievement," added Mr. Martin.

"Yes, with support and nurturing, he could be a very capable student," added Mr. Willows.

Then Mr. Martin looked directly at the boy. "Dexter, can you look me in the eye and tell me I stole your cell phone?"

Silence.

"Dexter, I'm waiting for your response. Look at me and answer my question."

"N-no, you didn't steal it." Then he broke down and sobbed. "I-I *am somebody*! I just want to be noticed by parents who know I exist." He continued sobbing inconsolably, reaching for a Kleenex tissue from the box on Mr. Willows' desk.

Mr. Martin stood up thinking. *Oh, dear God, how we have failed this child! We all had better get our priorities straight. This is one of the most disappointing displays of adult incompetence I've ever witnessed.*

"When everybody's ready to address the real problem and help this boy succeed, we should meet again," offered Mr. Martin. "I suggest we have a Student Study Team with Dexter, all his teachers, his parents, and Mr. Willows present."

Mr. Willows nodded in agreement. "Yes, I agree. We can set up an SST for next week."

Soon after the infamous meeting and the SST, Dexter was placed in foster care. Some investigating on Mr. Willows' part determined that Dexter spent most all his after-school hours and evenings on his own. His dad gave him some money each week to shift for himself and buy his own meals, but for the most part, he was an absentee father and once again, his mother "disappeared" from Dexter's life. Was it any wonder this child was so desperate for attention?

A young childless couple took Dexter into their home. His foster mother was very active in the community and her husband was a well-respected little league baseball coach who wasted no time in giving Dexter a position on the team. It looked as though a promising future was on the horizon for this former throwaway child.

Who Among You Would Serve?

Every day is spring while we're young.
None can refuse, time flies so fast,
Too dear to lose and too sweet to last.[1]

Though most likely conceived to immortalize lost love between a young man and woman, the lyrics above are no less significant when applied to countless students' devotion to a teacher and how their lives were drastically altered after having loved and lost their beloved mentor.

Ronald London was an eleventh grade U.S. history teacher. He was a dark-haired Marine veteran who fought early on in the war in Afghanistan, shortly after America was attacked on September 11, 2001. Having served three tours of duty, he was one of the lucky veterans who left the armed forces as a healthy and physically unscathed Lieutenant Colonel, though three tours must have taken a considerable mental toll on this tall, lanky Marine.

---

1   These lyrics by William Engvick were set to the enormously popular 1940's song by Alec Wilder and Morty Palitz.

Ronald London was a proud member of the new Greatest Generation, and like his predecessors of WW II, he rarely spoke of his experiences. Memories of erstwhile victories and horrors of losing men who fought beside him were his private domain. Maybe one day he'd share those memories with his own sons but for now, they remained preserved within this intensely private man. Ronald London chose to serve; he was not drafted. Unlike the days of the Vietnam War and both World Wars, service in the United States military is now entirely voluntary.

Boys and girls alike adored him. He possessed the qualities young girls yearned to have in the fathers who were absent from their lives or perhaps such qualities hoped for in their future husbands. To the boys, he was the best of role models who honored and served his country with distinction and who returned from war to serve his students with joy, enthusiasm, and respect. At a secondary school where a large percentage of students came from fatherless homes, he wielded a positive influence cherished among many of these adolescents. Girls had crushes on him; boys wanted to be like him.

When he taught, he didn't just lecture. He applied an endless variety of strategies to engage the kids and to, in turn, breathe life into our American past. He spent a week, for example, on the Transcontinental Railroad, built when the Panama Canal did not yet exist and during which time the American Civil War (1861-1865) was in progress under Lincoln's presidency. The timing itself was remarkable.

Regarding the transporting of building supplies from the east coast to the west coast, he made everyone chart the 18,000-mile journey by sea that took 202 days, starting in New York, sailing around Cape Horn, and finally docking in San Francisco.

He divided the class into Chinese and American laborers and made each group research how they lived on their work sites, what they ate and drank, and how they traveled to where they were supposed to lay the tracks. Those laborers building east-to-west and those building from west-to-east finally met at Promontory Summit in Utah to drive in the last spike made of gold, signifying completion of the project in 1869.

He taught the students about Leland Stanford, Charles Crocker, Mark Hopkins, and Collis Huntington, the major financial backers of the railroad, and Theodor Judah, master surveyor and heart and soul of this privately-funded project. It was supported by then-president, Abraham Lincoln, when the railroad was begun in 1861 and completed in 1869 with Andrew Johnson as president. It was a great oversight to Ronald London that the Transcontinental Railroad was never named the eighth wonder of the world.

When they studied the three branches of government, he turned the class into each of the three branches for a week at a time. They elected a president and vice president. Then they created the executive branch, complete with cabinet members. When they studied Congress, half the class became the House of Representatives; the other half operated as the Senate. Both houses had to undergo the process of creating and passing bills into law. When the class became the judicial branch, students conducted a trial that included witnesses subpoenaed from other classes, a jury, a defendant and plaintiff, defense and prosecuting attorneys, plaintiff, bailiff, sketch artist and recorder.

Kids loved coming to Mr. London's classes because they knew they would be actively engaged in some type of role-playing or research activity. He was *their* special teacher – former Lieutenant Colonel Ronald London – *their* Marine. Was it any wonder the boys looked up to him – literally, since he was six feet three inches tall – and the girls fantasized what it would be like to have a father or a husband like Mr. London?

Though Mr. London was beloved by all who knew him, he had an awakening one afternoon in his fifth period class that gave him pause for thought. They were studying World War II and reviewing the vocabulary pertaining to the unit. They came upon the word *conscription.*

"*Conscription?*" asked one of the boys. "What does that mean?"

"Anybody knows what this means?" asked their teacher.

Martin raised his hand; Mr. London nodded to him. "It means you are required to serve in the armed forces. You're drafted and have to serve."

"That's correct."

"Were you drafted, Mr. London?" a girl named Karina asked.

"No. We no longer have conscription. Our military is voluntary," he answered.

In disbelief, the same girl asked, "You mean you actually *volunteered* to go to war, to risk your life?"

"Since you put it that way, yes, I did; I volunteered to go to war."

"Why would you do that?" Karina persisted.

"The short answers is this: Countries don't defend themselves. Someone has to defend them when they're attacked. We were attacked on September 11th of 2001. If we stood idly by and did nothing, our attackers would possibly return to do us more harm. By taking the war overseas to our enemies, we keep them – hopefully – off of our soil."

Then he looked at the boys before him, remembering how young he was upon joining the Marines. He made the innocent mistake of asking, "Who among you would serve?"

Only Martin raised his hand. Others mumbled, "No way, not me." Or, "Couldn't pay me enough to do that." Or, "Not in *my* lifetime!"

The boys who admired and respected him had never made the connection between being a Marine and actually having to risk one's life in a war. This moment was an epiphany for them: Mr. London was not only a Marine; he fought in a war, put his life in danger, and most likely had to kill to defend himself against the enemy.

Then Karina raised her voice, berating the one boy who raised his hand. "Martin, why would you do such a risky, stupid thing? You're an idiot to go off to war. What are you thinking? Jeez, you're such a dork!"

A deadly silence fell over the stunned class. Then Martin said to Karina, "I would enlist because I want to be a Marine like Mr. London. Thanks to people like him, *you* can spout off your nonsense without getting your head blown off like you would in some other countries. Now just zip it, Miss Big-mouth!" Unlike Karina, Martin had a clear idea of what it meant to serve in any branch of the U.S. military.

The surprised Mr. London was not prepared to witness such strong feelings for and against the military among these young people. *I really opened Pandora's box; better put an end to the bickering*, he mused. *Maybe I was safer on the battlefield!*

"Well, Karina, if that's how you feel about Martin, that must be how you feel about me as well, and that's your right. That's part of what our armed forces do. We defend the Constitution and your right to speak your mind. However, it shouldn't be a matter of taking a stand for or against the military. It's more a matter of whether or not being in the military is one's calling, one's interest. The same logic would apply to any profession."

When some of her colleagues criticized Karina for being so outspoken, she gathered up her things and stalked out of the room. Mr. London called the office to have someone fetch the girl and take her to a place where she could cool off. She was a feisty redhead with a legendary temper, infamous among her peers.

All the joy in being with his students that period vaporized in those brief moments of hostile exchanges. *Tomorrow will be a better day, I'm sure,* he mused. The sadness didn't come from whether or not his students wanted to serve in the military, but rather from the mean-spirited attitudes with which they expressed differing opinions.

A few students tried to lighten the mood with reassuring comments such as, "Don't worry about Karina, Mr. London. She's always angry about something and doesn't know when to keep her mouth shut. It's like the world revolves around her."

"Yeah, she's not the only one with this problem," mumbled Martin, disappointed and shocked that none of his male peers shared his interest in the military.

Mr. London sat on the edge of his desk facing his beleaguered class, viewing them with sad turquoise blue eyes. He was trying to collect himself before addressing his concerns about their behavior. An uneasy silence fell over everyone. Finally, he spoke.

"In a short while, you will become the young adults of this country. You must decide what kind of Americans you want to be and where you want to see this country headed. There are many ways to serve your country, so each of you must determine how you wish to do that: teach, coach, preach, build, become great entrepreneurs like Bill Gates and the late Steve Jobs, serve in the armed forces, or whatever else you may choose. Being in the military is not the only way to serve your country." He paused, and concluded in a fatherly voice, "Just be sure that you love whatever you do. Find your passion and run with it."

"Is teaching *your* passion?" asked a boy in the front row.

"It was until this period," he teased. Everybody laughed.

"Yes," he continued, "I love teaching and look forward to coming to work each day. That's my hope for you, whatever you choose to do with your lives."

The bell rang and everyone somberly exited the room, some deep in thought as to what they would choose to do with their lives after high school or college, not to mention Martin who wanted to emulate his teacher by becoming a Marine. These kids who looked to Mr. London for positive mentoring had been given much to think about and for some, anticipating life after high school was a scary thing. They could only hope their choices would also lead to meaningful and fulfilling lives as they had for Mr. London.

Many students from his fifth period class went to sleep that night hoping they hadn't annoyed or angered him with their squabbles about serving in the military. Others were still pondering their futures. Time was running out on them, for they would soon be leaving their high school cocoon.

When everyone arrived on campus the next morning, some noticed the atmosphere was eerily quiet. Something didn't feel right about their campus, usually buzzing with chatty teenagers, the band practicing on the football field, some pick-up basketball games in progress on the outdoor courts, the usual hustle and bustle found on any high school campus.

Without warning, the principal's voice came over the loud speaker summoning everyone to the auditorium. No one had remembered any mention of a first-period assembly and one wasn't scheduled on the school's monthly calendar. Students were quizzically asking, "What's going on? What's the assembly about?"

They filed into the auditorium while teachers stood at each entrance making sure everyone headed quickly for a seat. On the dimly-lit stage were flowers, a podium with a microphone, a pair of tan military boots and a flag at half mast. The students from Mr. London's fifth period class frantically began seeking out each other. There was no doubt in their minds now why Dr. Washington summoned everybody to the auditorium. They clung to one another making their way to a row of empty seats. Karina timidly slipped in next to Martin, apologizing for her disparaging comments the day before.

"I'm so sorry for what I said yesterday. I don't know what gets into me when I say such stupid things. Please forgive me," she whispered.

"Apology accepted because I don't hold grudges," Martin smiled as he linked his arm through hers. "Brace yourself. I've a feeling we're in for some really bad news." Karina nodded in agreement.

When everyone was in place and quiet, the weary principal, Dr. Washington, emerged from backstage, stepped up to the podium and hesitantly began speaking into the microphone after clearing his throat. He was a short and slender stylishly dressed African-American in his early fifties. The stress on his face undermined the good looks of a man who, under normal circumstances, looked much younger than his years.

He spoke haltingly, attempting to keep his emotions in check. "Today . . . I have some very sad news to share . . . I thought it would be best . . . if – if everyone heard it at the same time . . . Mr. London – formerly addressed as Lieutenant Colonel Ronald London – was killed in an automobile accident last night . . . run off an overpass by a drunk driver . . ."

Gasps went up from the audience while Dr. Washington held his hand up to quiet them before continuing. "Both died on the spot of their injuries. Lieutenant Colonel Ronald London . . . is survived by his wife and three young sons. It is ironic that he served three tours of duty thousands of miles away, yet was killed just a few miles from his home. We have lost . . . a great teacher, role model and friend; America has lost a distinguished veteran who served his country with honor. The family will let us know about arrangements for the – for the memorial service. I'm so sorry to be the one to tell you this, for I know how beloved he was by all the students and faculty here. Please stand now while our band director, Mr. Sanchez, plays *Taps* in Mr. London's honor."

Students arose, some in shock, some crying, others clinging to their peers as Mr. Sanchez played *Taps*. Following the musical tribute, they sat, too stunned to move. "We have grievance counselors on hand," offered Dr. Washington, "for anyone who would like to meet with one, either individually or in small groups. In a few minutes the bell will ring to report to your first period classes. Meanwhile, please remain here and honor Mr. London in complete silence."

Dr. Washington remained on the stage, head bowed. The students did as he asked, aware that not a sound could be heard throughout the auditorium. Their heads were either bowed or resting on a friend's shoulder while others had their eyes riveted on the empty tan boots and flag at half-mast.

When the bell finally rang, everyone disbursed like heart-broken zombies headed for class. Those who didn't know this Marine-turned-teacher were devastated for having been denied the opportunity of taking a class from this legendary history teacher. Those who knew him felt the exquisite pain of his loss.

As for the fifth period classmates who spent their final hour with him marred by dissension, their sorrow was perhaps the greatest, for during those few thoughtless minutes, minutes that could never be taken back, explained, or vindicated, they sensed how disappointed he must have been in them, or worse, how disappointed they were in themselves. True, they were young and sometimes foolish, but they were also capable of feeling remorseful and apologetic for their insensitive and immature behavior when Lieutenant Colonel Ronald London asked of them this simple question: "Who among you would serve?"

A Tale of Two Twins

"M-O-O-O-M! Have you seen my cell phone? I left it on my nightstand, but it's not here. Have you seen it?" Jimmy called from his upstairs bedroom.

"Yes, I saw it," she answered back while moving closer to the stairs, "but you are not getting it back until you clean your room. You were supposed to pick up your stuff and put it away three days ago. Honestly, I don't know how you can live in that rubble."

"I'm used to it. It's *my* room, so what difference does it make if it's clean or not?"

"Have you seen your brother's room? It's spotless; everything has a place. And by the way, you left your phone in the kitchen, not on your nightstand."

"Well, I really need it and I don't have any time to clean my room before football practice tonight. Pleeease may I have it? I promise I'll clean my room after practice."

"This topic is not open for negotiation," answered Mrs. Templeton, picking up a stray hand towel thrown over the back of a chair while heading toward the dining room. "Suit yourself. You're not getting it back until your room is clean and that's final," she responded.

Jimmy knew his mother meant what she said. Like it or not, both parents were consistent when it came to disciplining their children. He stalked downstairs and headed toward the kitchen where Mrs. Templeton was preparing dinner.

"Since I wasted so much time looking for my phone," Jimmy snapped at his mother, "I won't have time to eat before practice. This is all *your* stupid fault!" he exclaimed eyeing his mother with a dramatic flare so typical among teens when they are exasperated.

"Whoa, whoa, *whoa!*" Called out Mr. Templeton from the family room. "Don't you *ever* address your mother in that angry tone of voice. Understand?"

"Understood. Sorry," he mumbled.

Just then, Larry entered giving Jimmy a playful sock on the arm. "Hey, what's up?"

Silence.

"Dude, you look like you just lost your best friend . . . that would be your phone, right?"

Jimmy glared back, not amused by the joke.

Larry looked quizzically at their mom, "Did you take Jimmy's phone again?" Not waiting for her response, he looked back at his brother and continued, "Seriously, Dude, you've gotta cut back on texting and do time in the real world. Don't you ever get sick of texting?"

"I am so done with this conversation," retorted Jimmy. "I'm outa here . . . be back around 10:00." He stalked out, grabbing a couple of dinner rolls along the way.

After Jimmy stormed out, Larry looked blankly at his mother. "Yikes! What brought that on?"

"He's ticked off because I won't return his phone until he cleans his room. I worry about him because he has such a hard time relating to real people. Hopefully, something positive will come of his love for technology. Right now, all he does is text. I doubt this skill will bring him to the forefront among the movers and shakers in technology," she sighed with a hint of sarcasm in her voice.

"Jeez! I haven't even *seen* my phone for three days, let alone used it. I have no idea where it is. If Jimmy finds my cell, I'll never see it again. I'd much rather create stories or write articles for the school paper than text. Honestly, English will become extinct one day because of all the texting lingo. Nobody spells anything any more."

"Well, at least he's smart, so hopefully his intelligence will lead him to a successful path, whatever that may be."

"Actually, Mom, Jimmy knows a great deal about technology. Everyone at Monrovia High comes to him for help, including the teachers, whenever they're stumped or when something doesn't work right. He was even called out of class the other day to fix the DVD player in Mr. Simpson's room. He's just addicted to texting, that's all."

"Good to hear he's needed around school. At least helping others gets him interacting with people. It probably makes him feel a bit special, too."

Larry continued, appearing not to have heard his mother's last comments. "It's a wonder any of us learned to spell. Let's take the word C-L-E-A-N, for example. How many ways do we see it spelled in advertising? We see C-L-E-E-N, K-L-E-E-N,

K-L-E-A-N, C-L-E-N-E, K-L-E-N-E, and so on. We never see consistent, correct spelling any more. Drives me nuts."

For one so social minded, Larry could also worry about things that would never occur to most teenagers. But again, writing was his passion, so he considered it his job to worry about such things.

"You should see the way some of the articles look when kids on the staff turn them in for editing. Yikes! I sure wish we had L'Académie Française in this country. In French class we learned the Academy was established in the 17th century to prevent the desecration of their language and maintain its purity so that foreign words wouldn't creep into it. Even today, print media is fined for misspellings and use of foreign words that aren't italicized to indicate they're not part of the French language."

"Maybe you should start L'Académie Monrovainne," his father joked in his best French accent.

"Ha! Ha! Seriously, our language is in big trouble," Larry complained.

Indeed, nobody could deny Larry's over-the-top passion for English. He defended its preservation with the protective intensity for which animal rights' groups are known.

True, the twins could not have been more different in interests, personality and temperament. With the exception of their identical physical appearance, they may just as well have come from different families. Both were tall, Irish-looking lads with dark hair, brown eyes, and pale, lightly-freckled skin. This is where their likenesses ended.

Larry was definitely a child of the real world who depended heavily upon his tech-savvy brother when it came to formatting essays, research projects, and graph work for various classes. However, he had always wished that Jimmy were more social, more interested in doing things together. Unlike most twins who have symbiotic relationships, these brothers did very few things together. Being on the varsity football team was the only interactive endeavor that held Jimmy's interest. To his credit, at least he wasn't a complete recluse and the exercise kept him in great physical condition.

On the other hand, gregarious Larry was nicknamed "Mr. Social" because he was involved in so many organizations where he consistently put his leadership skills to good use. He was well liked by teachers and peers and was completely connected to high school campus life. However, his extra-curricular pursuits never interfered with his academic progress. Larry had enough energy to keep both worlds running at full pitch.

There was another troubling difference between the twins. It was that dreaded time in every college-bound senior's life to start the application process with endless forms to fill out and essays to compose. Because Larry had a passion for writing, he had honed his skills as the newspaper editor for three of his four years on the staff. He wrote expository articles, interviews, some advice columns, and even a few short stories. In fact, Larry's love for writing prepared him not only for the college application process, but also morphed into a marketable skill. He already had a part-time job lined up with a local newspaper for winter and spring breaks as well as the summer following graduation.

Texting, on the other hand, did not lead to anything but more texting for Jimmy. In vain, he struggled with his college essays. Although Larry helped him to organize his ideas and corrected the flawed grammar and spelling, there was little content to edit. For the past four years, Jimmy had produced the barest minimum regarding dreaded required essay assignments. To that end, he was not on "friendly terms" with concepts such as deep critical thought and elaboration. This circumstance led to little more than extended text messages with all the words spelled out (no abbreviations) for his college essays.

One late afternoon when Jimmy was at football practice, Larry shared what he thought was a brilliant idea with his parents who were chatting in the family room over glasses of wine.

"I've been thinking about Jimmy and wondering if college is the best plan for him," he began.

"What do you mean by that?" asked Mr. Templeton, taking a sip from his glass.

"Have you looked at his college essays?"

"No, he never showed them to us, but that's not unusual for him. He rarely lets us see his work," responded Mr. Templeton.

Larry continued, "They totally suck. I mean seriously; they suck. I'm not saying that just to be critical or mean, and I don't want to discourage him, but it just doesn't seem like college is the right choice for him." He walked over to the counter of the adjacent kitchen, grabbed some cookies and poured himself a glass of chocolate milk. "I've tried to help him, but there's just no content there and I think it's because he's not committed to getting a college education. At a trade or tech school, he could really shine and develop his skills."

"So, Larry, what do you propose for your brother?" asked his mother. "It's true, you have always been the family academician, whereas Jimmy has always been more of a hands-on type."

"Exactly!" Larry exclaimed, returning to the family room with his cookies and milk. "My English teacher would call him a tactile or kinesthetic learner. In order for ideas to sink in, he needs to be physically connected to them. That explains why he's so good with computers. He's never been comfortable in social situations and academics just aren't his thing, but give him a hands-on project and he's all over it."

"You think he'd do better in a trade/tech situation to further his education after high school?"

"I do. But also, I'd like to try something at school such as a joint project where we can combine our talents. Dad, would you be willing to let him use your new video cam with the capacity to shoot still photos so we can create a photo-journal project for the yearbook?"

"Depends on where you're doing the shooting. I'm not wild about him bringing my expensive camera to school where it may get lost. What kind of project did you have in mind, Son?"

"A couple of kids on the yearbook staff said they were looking for someone to create a senior project about our city of Monrovia. They need a photographer and someone to do the write-up. They want to dedicate the annual to the city and thank everyone for our new campus, paid for by the taxpayers. It would be a unique way to show our appreciation for the sacrifices they made so we could have a state-of-the-art campus. I mean, what other school has an auditorium that any professional theater group would envy?"

"This would be an after-school project?" Mr. Templeton inquired.

"For sure. Football season is nearly over, so the timing's perfect. We can get started right away. Our faculty adviser will give us weekend access to the campus for our project, so only a day's worth of videotaping would be completed during school hours. I'm hoping that maybe Jimmy could give up texting for part of each day, so together we could create something of value for our high school and the community," Larry explained.

"Sounds like a noble endeavor for you boys. Your mother and I are two of those Monrovia taxpayers," he smiled, "so we'd appreciate such a gesture of thanks along with everyone else in town."

"You'll let us use the video cam, then?"

"Sure, but just be careful. Have you discussed this with Jimmy?"

"Not yet, but I will this weekend after his last game. Besides, I wanted to run this idea by you first."

"Well, you have our blessing," smiled Mrs. Templeton. "It sounds like you've put a lot of thought into this."

"I have. It would be awesome for him to experience how it feels to create something of tangible value to benefit others, rather than sending texts that are most likely deleted five seconds after they're read. His awesome talent should be part of our high school history," he said wistfully.

"Not to mention yours," they added.

Larry stood up, carrying his empty glass and plate to the dishwasher. "Gotta get started on this project now so there will be something to show Jimmy when I make my pitch. Thanks for letting us use your camera. Pray for me," he smiled. "If he agrees, he'll probably need some form of texting rehab, especially if he chooses a cluttered room over getting his cell back," he chuckled.

"We'll look around for some twelve-step programs," his mother joked. "Meanwhile, dinner will be ready in about an hour, so stick around."

"Copy that," Larry acknowledged as he bounded up the stairs, headed for his room.

Both boys knew how lucky they were to have such support-ive parents. They didn't always agree with their positions on issues, but they appreciated having a mother and father who were there for them and who made them feel it was all right to discuss anything about their lives without put-downs or repri-mands. They relished what Larry always called their "house-hold harmony," an atmosphere of mutual love and respect.

The Sunday following Monrovia's final game of the season against San Marino, Larry approached Jimmy who was by the pool, basking in the Southern California sunshine.

"Are you glad football's over now? You played a great game last night. You should have heard Mom and Dad cheering you on. Must have been a really good feeling to win the final game, right?" ventured Larry. "I can't imagine how proud you must have felt."

"Totally. Yeah, it was cool. Now I'll have more time to work on those college essays. I've run out of excuses, so I've gotta get 'em done. I've also gotta get some of my grades up."

"Do you know your overall GPA?"

"I think it's barely a 2.00, something like that."

"So Jimmy, may I ask you something about college?"

"Yeah, what?"

"Are you sure you really want to go? I mean are you just going through the motions of applying because I'm doing it or because you think Mom and Dad expect both of us to go? From reading your essays, it just seems like your heart isn't in it."

Jimmy suddenly sat up. "So what're you saying? You think I'm too stupid to apply for college? That I'm just a dumb jock who can only text and play ball?"

"No, chill, Dude! Jeez! I'm not saying that at all. Your knowledge of technology goes way beyond texting and you know it. You're a creative hands-on kind of guy who could have a brilliant future in technology. That's *your* gift, your passion. Also, I just think you may not be happy in an academic situation loaded down with books to read and papers to write. It would be more of the same – to a greater degree – of the work you loathe doing in high school."

"Jeez, Larry! Have you got the next four years of my life planned out for me? Have you written job résumés for me? Trade school applications? What do you suggest I do with the rest of my life, Larry, since you're so bloody smart?"

Well, this is going well, Larry thought. *I should have kept my mouth shut and let him discover for himself that none of his sucky essays would ever see the light of day among members of any college admissions board.*

"C'mon, Mr. Brain, I'm asking for your suggestions. You seem to know what's best for me," Jimmy persisted.

"Okay, Dude, just calm down! Here's the deal. Does it make sense for you to continue doing for the next four years what you've hated doing here the past three and a half years? Your passion is *technology*, not academia, so why not follow your heart and focus on what you love . . . on your passion? You've been so caught up in the virtual world that you haven't given any thought to what will happen to you in the real world after graduation. That's all I'm saying."

Jimmy sat motionless, trying to process what his brother had just explained. True, he hadn't given any thought to his future until now, and he dreaded the thought of picking up where he left off on the college application process. He was also aware that Larry had already submitted his applications to USC, UC Berkeley, Stanford, Loyola Marymount, and UCLA. He knew that his essays were exquisitely-written works of art. How did he know this? He snuck into Larry's room one night and read them, hoping to get some inspiration for his own compositions. They only made him feel all the more hopeless and inadequate. The more he thought about his brother's reasoning, the more sense it made.

"I'm going to let that sink in," Larry interjected. "For now, all I'm asking is that you look at your essays and if, after reading them, you can tell me you have a burning desire for college, I'll keep my mouth shut. If, on the other hand, you think it would be wiser to explore your giftedness and go with training in some area of technology, I have an exit strategy that would allow both of us to go forth from Monrovia High School in a blaze of glory."

He waved his arm ceremoniously and took a deep bow at the end of his sentence. "And now, Sir Textalot, I shall leave you with this thought: Steve Jobs and Bill Gates did not have college degrees and nobody thought they were stupid." He gave another deep bow and started toward the house.

"Hey, wait! Not so fast!" called Jimmy. "What's your exit strategy?"

"You'll have to wait; I'm not telling you right now. Just reread your essays and think about what I said. Not all wildly success-ful people have college educations. We'll talk again in a couple of days about my plan," Larry advised. "Now I smell bread coming out of the oven, so I'm going to take my leave and sample a few pieces. Let's hear it for our mother who can bake up a storm!" In an instant he was gone, leaving Jimmy alone with his thoughts.

The following Tuesday, Jimmy knocked on Larry's bed-room door. "May I come in?" he asked.

"No, get out! . . . *Just kidding!* C'mon in."

Jimmy began, "I was thinking about everything you said Sunday regarding me and college. If my grades were better, I could focus on technology at a regular four-year college. But that's not possible because they suck."

"Well, even if they didn't, I still think you'd be miserable in a four-year college or university because there would be no let up on all that other stuff you don't like. It would keep you away from what you really want to do. That's why Steve Jobs dropped out of college. He was bored to tears and wanted to focus only on areas that interested him. Look where that path took him. Jobs literally changed the way the world communicates. Like him, you've gotta find your own way," Larry advised. "Look, you and I are pretty bright guys, but our talents just happen to lie in different areas."

"You're pretty convincing."

"It's my job. That's what I do because I'm Mr. Social, and I boss people around." He gave Jimmy a playful push on both shoulders. "Just stick with me, kid."

"Okay, so what's this mysterious plan you were talking about? How are we going to leave Monrovia High School in 'a blaze of glory,' as you put it?"

Larry proceeded to explain the project, while Jimmy enthusiastically nodded from time to time. When Larry finished, Jimmy jumped right in with ideas flowing like water from a burst dam. Their project was officially launched right there in Larry's bedroom. They talked and planned for the next few hours, two brothers connecting more closely than they had at any other time in their lives.

When Mr. and Mrs. Templeton clicked off the television, they could hear the boys' animated discussion in full swing upstairs. By then, it was nearly 11:30.

"I'd better remind them it's time to get to bed," said Mrs. Templeton.

"No, wait. Let them talk as long as they want tonight. They are obviously on a roll. I suspect that Jimmy bought into Larry's joint yearbook project. Let's let them be for now. They're young, so one night of missed sleep won't hurt them."

"You're right," agreed Mrs. Templeton. "All too soon, they'll be going their separate ways, living God knows how far apart. They should enjoy their final months together."

"Agreed. We old folks, however, need our beauty rest," he chuckled, "so let's turn in now." He called upstairs, "Good night, boys; see you in the morning."

"Okay, copy that," called Larry. "Can you wake us up at 6:30?"

"Will do," answered their father.

During the next couple of months, the boys worked feverishly on their project. From time to time, Larry would leak out tidbits of information in The Wildcat (school newspaper), hoping his teasers would entice the kids to purchase yearbooks. His plan, including flyers created, printed and distributed by the yearbook staff, worked. Sales went through the roof. The entire student body was invited to sign the "Thank-You" page in the annual so of course, most everyone wanted to see their signatures in print and have a hand in showing their appreciation to the community. That was part of Larry's successful buy-in strategy.

Shortly before the yearbook was to be published, Jimmy suggested, "Why don't I edit the video that includes parts of your text narrated in your own voice, and combine it with great music so we'd have a multimedia show?"

"Sweet! We'll rock this assembly!" Larry exclaimed as they high-fived each other. "I'll ask Mr. Anderson for permission to schedule it. This gig would be our final plug for yearbook sales. I bet we could get close to one hundred per cent participation. We're not far from that now."

"Game on! How can the head honcho refuse your request?" Jimmy laughed.

The assembly was planned to take place the day before annuals were scheduled for distribution. When D-Day finally arrived, the students poured excitedly into the newly-remodeled auditorium. There had been so much hype about the assembly and annual, so of course, everyone was expecting to be royally entertained.

As expected, the Brothers Templeton did let them down. After the show, everyone cheered and applauded, some standing, some sitting, but all clapping with pride and appreciation for how the twins had pulled off transforming a portion of the annual into a festive multimedia extravaganza. When Mr. Anderson brought them on the stage to be acknowledged, the boys were filled with pride, taking in the appreciation of faculty and peers.

"Enjoy this while we can," whispered Larry. "This won't last forever."

What the boys did not know at the time was that their parents were in the audience. The principal was so impressed with their rehearsals, he called the Templetons and invited them to slip into the balcony where they'd be unnoticed by their sons. Mr. Templeton arranged his schedule so he could leave work early and attend the afternoon assembly. He and his wife left immediately afterward, letting their sons bask in glory among their adoring peers and admiring faculty.

When the auditorium had emptied, the boys remained behind to strike the show and tidy up around the stage and light controls. Then they sat cross-legged on the floor to let it all sink in, just the two of them enjoying this moment of closeness, alone in an empty auditorium, silently soaking in the afterglow of success.

"I can't believe we pulled this thing off!" exclaimed Jimmy, elated with his successful venture out of the virtual world.

"I can. There was never a doubt in my mind you could rock this place. Didn't I say a couple of months ago how gifted you are with technology and that you're not one of the dullest knives in the drawer just because you aren't cut out for academia? With the right training, networking, and connections, you'll have a brilliant future in this business. Who knows? I may be standing in line one day waiting for your autograph," Larry smiled, standing up to bow deeply before his brother again in mock admiration for a royal being.

"I know that none of this would have happened without your constant support and encouragement, so thanks for getting up in my business and talking sense into me," said the grateful brother.

"My pleasure. Like I said, it's my job to bend humanity to my will," he smiled. "By the way, what happened to your cell? I haven't seen you use it for ages."

"I never got it back from Mom. I figured by never cleaning my room, she wouldn't return it and I wouldn't be tempted to use it. This also gave me a good excuse to explain to my friends why I wasn't texting. The blame game – sorry Mom – really worked well. Besides, when would I have had time to use it since pairing up with you on this project?"

"Ah, yes, my ulterior motive exposed at last!"

They gave one another playful socks on the arm, gathered up their things, and exited the auditorium in which they had "rocked the house" with their multimedia preview of the yearbook dedicated to the community of Monrovia.

Giddy with excitement, the boys burst through the front door with a cheery, "We're h-o-o-o-o-me!"

"Hi, guys! We're in the family room so come join us," called Mr. Templeton.

When the boys appeared, wreathed in smiles, their mom asked with a knowing glance at her husband, "So how did your assembly go, guys? Was it a hit?"

"Mom, Dad, it was awesome," exclaimed Jimmy. "Everybody loved it. They cheered and applauded for what seemed like forever when it was over." Larry stood silently by, beaming with pride as his brother carried on.

Mr. Templeton turned slyly to his wife, "Should we let them in on our little secret?" She nodded in the affirmative.

"Boys, we have a confession to make. We attended the assembly at the invitation of Mr. Anderson. He was so impressed with rehearsals that he invited us to see your presentation. We slipped into the balcony so you wouldn't see us."

The boys stood with their mouths agape. Finally, Jimmy stammered, "S-so you were there? You saw the whole show?"

"The whole thing, and we couldn't be prouder," beamed their father. "It's rather obvious that you are both very gifted in your own ways, so whatever paths you choose, success will follow as long as you stick with your passions."

"You'd better be prepared for some more adulation tomorrow when the annuals are distributed," advised their mom. "I suspect you'll be further inundated with adoring fans wanting your autographs. Just make sure each of you has several pens on hand." Then she looked at Jimmy with a mischievous twinkle in her eye. "As for you, Jimmy, do I hang on to your phone and continue cleaning around the things strewn about your room?"

"Yeah," he smiled sheepishly. "You've been my alibi for not texting my friends, so if you don't mind, just hold onto it until after graduation. I've gotten to enjoy living in the real world; it certainly has its rewards." Everybody laughed.

Meanwhile, Larry had been accepted to all the colleges of his choice except USC. He chose Stanford University up north in Palo Alto, California. Jimmy had put together a demo DVD of the multimedia show. He sent a copy to Otis Institute of Art and Design, America's first independent, fully accredited school of art, located in Los Angeles. He also sent one to Cogswell Polytechnical College in Sunnyvale, in northern California's Silicon Valley. Cogswell's web site boasted "a unique blend of hands-on, project-based learning and developing critical thinking skills . . . designed to produce industry leaders." There couldn't have been a more perfect match for Jimmy, for the Silicon Valley has always been a hotbed of technological achievement.

Finally, high school had come to an end. Yearbooks were signed and mercifully, final exams were memories of the past. It was time for the graduating seniors to shine before a proud gathering of parents, friends, and relatives. Graduation ceremonies on the Monrovia High School football field, complete with an honor guard, were always dignified and lovely occasions. The field was set against a breathtaking backdrop of the majestic San Gabriel Mountains, a range that runs from northern Los Angeles County to western San Bernardino County. They underwent a mesmerizing change of color as the sun sank behind them and the field lights came on, taking over where the setting sun left off.

The Templetons were overcome with pride as their twin sons were called up not individually, but as a pair. Perhaps Mr. Anderson made this decision because they were twins, or because of their blockbuster success as multimedia rock stars. Whatever his reason, the graduates and audience broke out in prolonged applause, while chanting alternately, "Jimmy, Larry! Jimmy, Larry!"

As for Jimmy's post-graduation plans, both art institutes accepted his application. Predictably, he chose Cogswell in Sunnyvale because of its close proximity to where his brother would be at Stanford in Palo Alto. Their newly-formed alliance was cemented in a bond of recent success that neither brother wanted severed by physical distance between two institutions of higher learning.

To the relief and joy of the Templetons, their sons were ready to move on with the next phase of their lives. Each had found his passion that would surely provide clear-cut direction and fulfillment for many years to come.

What could be better for all graduating seniors than a productive past pointing to a promising future?

Nothing. Absolutely nothing.

Acknowledgements

My deepest gratitude and thanks go to Robert Montes, who generously allowed me to take over his class one day a week for a semester in order to "teen test" this collection of short stories in our Meet the Author Project.

Appreciation goes to my new BFFs from his Spring 2012 Freshman English class at Monrovia High School: Dherik Ahmad, Allen Campos, Katelin Casner, Brenda Evangs, Preston Guerrero, Alfredo Maciel, Angelica Malone, Gabriel Martinez, Nicholas Miranda, Aranza Osario, Alicia Rangel, Julian Rodriguez, Mia Romero, Taylor Smith, Margaret Szavoszt, Brandon Villaflores, plus fifteen others who wished to remain anonymous. I am grateful for their interest, support, suggestions, and the eagle eyes that caught typos along the way.

Thanks and appreciation must also go to former Deputy Superintendent and my beloved Boss Lady for ten years, Dr. Debby Collins, whose suggestion it was to apply for a grant from the Monrovia Schools Foundation in order to fund class copies of the manuscript. Lucky for me, this organization thought it was a worthy project for which I am most grateful. Thank you to my efficient contact source, Bruce Staller, who handled the details.

To former Principal Darvin Jackson of Monrovia High School (now Assistant Superintendent and my new Boss Man), I offer thanks and praise for allowing us the freedom to try something new.

To the parents who "produced" these vibrant young teenagers, thank you for your contributions to my joy and pleasure in working with your children. They reminded me of why I love to do what I was born to do: teach.

To my editor, Scott Lyness, USC statistician and research associate, thank you so much for all of your suggestions and insights shared during our late-night phone conversations. Thank you for setting me straight when my own point of view or "voice" impeded the progress of a story. You have helped me to know the difference between a teacher's and a writer's hat and for that I am most grateful.

Finally, to author, Dennis Sanchez, I can't thank you enough for your mentoring on technical issues. Your knowledge, advice, technical editing, and time invested in the styling and formatting of the manuscript has been of invaluable help to me.

Also by Linda Jones Simmons

This
Was
Meant
to Be

How Loss and Vulnerability
Generate Passion and Success

◆ LINDA JONES SIMMONS ◆

Printed in Great Britain
by Amazon

66216109R00083